# PROMISES OF SPRING

Sophie, who's in between jobs and recovering from a broken relationship, offers to help out her Aunt Rose in Kent. Reluctantly, she finds herself being drawn into village affairs. Keir Ellison, a neighbour, is heavily involved in plans for a Craft Centre, but there is much opposition from the older residents who have different ideas for the old chapel. Sophie is attracted to Keir, but soon realises he's a man of mystery. Can she trust him?

MS

JEAN M. LONG

---

# PROMISES OF SPRING

## Complete and Unabridged

## LINFORD
*Leicester*

First published in Great Britain in 2011

First Linford Edition
published 2013

British Library CIP Data

Long, Jean M.
   Promises of spring.- -
   (Linford romance library)
   1. Love stories.
   2. Large type books.
   I. Title II. Series
   823.9'14–dc23

   ISBN 978–1–4448–1397–5

Published by
F. A. Thorpe (Publishing)
Anstey, Leicestershire

Set by Words & Graphics Ltd.
Anstey, Leicestershire
Printed and bound in Great Britain by
T. J. International Ltd., Padstow, Cornwall

This book is printed on acid-free paper

# Meeting a Neighbour

Sophie Burnett slowed to a crawl, as a sudden flurry of snow made driving even more hazardous. She must have been mad to have attempted the journey to Penbridge that day, but she'd got no intention of letting Aunt Rose down.

A couple of days ago there had been a brief message left on the answer-phone from a neighbour, informing the Burnetts that the elderly lady had sprained her ankle badly.

After a brief family confab, Sophie had volunteered to stay with Aunt Rose in Kent for a week or so.

'Under any other circumstances, I'd have been more than happy to go myself,' Sophie's mother had said. 'But June and Colin have been good friends for such a long time, so your father and I can't possibly miss their ruby wedding

1

party this weekend. Rose insisted she's coping well when I spoke to her on the phone yesterday, but you know how fiercely independent she is. Reading between the lines, I think she's putting on a brave face and could do with some help.'

Sophie's brother, Tim, had already gone skiing with his girlfriend, so there really was no-one else.

Sophie peered ahead. Rose Cottage had got to be around here somewhere, but all she could make out, stretching into the distance, was a sea of white with no sign of habitation.

After a few minutes, the snow eased, and Sophie inched her way gingerly forward, in what she hoped was the right direction. Rose Cottage had always been a bit tricky to find.

Even in the best of weather it had been easy to miss the turning and, previously, Sophie had been driven there by her father.

To her relief, she suddenly saw a couple of ragstone cottages set back from the road and pulled in as near as she could.

A sharp rap on the window nearly made her jump out of her skin. A man peered at her with a pair of intense brown eyes, mouthing something.

She wound down the window a crack, hoping he wasn't about to attack her.

'At last! Rose sent me to see if there was any sign of you. We thought you'd have been here long ago.'

'In case it's escaped your notice, it's been snowing heavily,' she rejoined, unable to make out much about the man, apart from the fact that he was quite large, probably in his thirties, and swathed in a thick jacket with a hood.

'Well, you're here now — you'll have to park round the back.' He directed her, waving his arms about in the process.

It was slow going and Sophie was greatly relieved when she'd finally reached the spot he'd indicated.

By the time she'd locked the car and retrieved some of her luggage from the boot, the man had reappeared.

'I'm Rose's neighbour, from Rowan-bank,' he told her tersely, taking the suitcase from her, and leaving her to follow as best she could with the bags. 'She was expecting to spend the New Year with you and your family. By the time I'd returned from visiting friends, she was in a bit of a state. She'd gone out to find her cat, and slipped and sprained her ankle badly. It's a good job it wasn't any worse. Goodness knows how she'd managed to get back indoors. Anyway, I took her to A & E just to be on the safe side.'

'Well, you're obviously a good neighbour,' Sophie told him, thinking it was typical of Daphne to have backed out of having her aunt to stay over the New Year. Sophie knew that Rose had been greatly looking forward to visiting her late husband's niece and she hadn't told the Burnetts she'd been on her own over the holiday after all.

'It's just as well I came back when I did. Your aunt's been housebound ever since,' the neighbour told Sophie, a note of reproach in his voice.

Sophie didn't bother to correct him. After all, it was an easy enough mistake to make to assume that she was Rose's niece. She was freezing cold and her toes and fingers were numb. No, explanations could wait until later.

\* \* \*

Aunt Rose's face lit up when Sophie came into the kitchen, reassuring her that she'd made the right decision in coming here. Sophie kissed the elderly lady's cheek and commiserated over the sprained ankle, all the time aware of the man leaning against the Welsh dresser observing her. She registered that he was largish with broad shoulders.

He had pushed the hood of his anorak back to reveal thick fair hair flopping forward over his brow and she could see that he had a firm, angular jawline and rugged good looks.

'I didn't think you'd manage to get

here in all this bad weather. What a day!' Aunt Rose said.

'I did try to phone you, but I'm afraid I couldn't get a signal,' Sophie told her.

'Well, never mind. I'm so pleased to see you. Would you like to freshen up? Keir's made us some soup, although I'm afraid I've had mine already. I've put you in the back bedroom. Fortunately, Keir's lent me his cleaning lady, so the room's ready and the bed's aired. She couldn't come in today, of course.'

'I'll bring your case,' Keir said, and Sophie followed him back into the tiny hall and up the narrow stairs.

'How on earth is Aunt Rose managing to get up here?'

'She isn't. We've made up a bed for her on the bed-settee in the dining room for the time being, and fortunately she's got the downstairs cloakroom, so she can manage perfectly well.' He paused and pushed open a door.

'Anyway, here you are. It's a pleasant room.'

'Thanks for everything,' she said, meeting a pair of cool, brown eyes. 'It's good to know someone's been keeping an eye on Aunt Rose.'

'Yes, well, what are neighbours for?' he said briefly. 'She's a lovely lady and it's a great pity her family don't appreciate her more.'

Sophie felt that the criticism was somehow directed at her and decided to put him straight.

'Actually, Aunt Rose doesn't have any close family living, apart from her husband's niece, Daphne, and a couple of elderly cousins in Shropshire.'

Keir frowned. 'But I thought — so you're not related to Daphne?'

She shook her head. 'Most definitely not! I'm Sophie — Sophie Burnett. Aunt Rose isn't really my aunt at all. She was my father's cousin's sister-in-law. Uncle Hugh lived at Rowanbank.'

She was gratified to see that Keir looked slightly awkward.

'Right — well, I'm sorry for the misunderstanding — must have got my wires crossed. I found your phone number in Rose's address book, listed under D. Burnett and assumed . . . '

'That's my father, David Burnett. His cousin, Hugh, lived at Rowanbank, until he died last year, as I'm sure you're aware. Uncle Hugh's first wife, Mary, was Aunt Rose's twin sister.'

'Yes, of course — it all makes sense now.' He stretched out a hand. 'I'm Keir Ellison, Miss Burnett. I moved into Rowanbank last summer.'

Her fingers tingled as they made contact with his. She had to admit he was a seriously attractive man. For a moment, their eyes met and then she lowered her gaze, feeling oddly disturbed.

'I'll go and heat up that soup,' he told her. 'Ready in ten minutes.'

Sophie barely had time to remove her wet anorak, towel and brush her damp hair and have a quick wash. Her head was in a whirl.

Sophie and her family hadn't realised anyone had moved into Rowanbank.

They'd assumed the neighbour who'd left the message had been someone from the adjacent cottage.

Sophie crossed to the small lattice window and peered out, but the view was practically obliterated by a blanket of snow. It was at least a couple of years since she'd last been here, but her parents had stayed with Aunt Rose when they'd attended Hugh's funeral last year.

After her sister, Mary, had died, Aunt Rose had helped keep house for her brother-in-law, Hugh, but then, right out of the blue, many years later he'd remarried and his second wife, Erica, had made it abundantly clear that Rose was no longer welcome at Rowanbank. Soon after Hugh had died, Erica had gone abroad.

A few minutes later, Sophie was seated in Aunt Rose's small kitchen with a steaming bowl of soup in front of her and a plate of sandwiches.

'Aren't you going to stay for a cup of tea, Keir?' Rose asked, as he got to his feet. 'Surely your class will be cancelled tonight?'

'Yes, I expect so, but I'll leave you two to catch up. You must have a lot to talk about so I'll say goodbye for now.'

And he was gone. For a large man he moved quickly, Sophie thought, wondering fleetingly how old he was.

Aunt Rose set down her cup. 'Keir has been very good to me. I couldn't wish for a better neighbour.'

Sophie took a spoonful of soup. It was wonderfully warming.

'Did he really make this soup?'

'He's a man of many talents and is quite capable of looking after himself with a little help from Mavis Briggs, his cleaning lady.'

'Mrs Briggs! She was Uncle Hugh's cleaning lady too, wasn't she? I used to play with her daughter, Crystal, when I stayed at Rowanbank as a child. We've kept in touch ever since.'

'Goodness knows what state that house would have been in without Mavis and her husband keeping an eye on it all those weeks it was standing empty.'

'I'm surprised Erica didn't stay there until it was sold.'

'Oh, it was as if she couldn't wait to shake the dust of Penbridge from her heels. She cleared off abroad almost as soon as it was decently possible. Anyway, Keir's at Rowanbank now and I couldn't be more pleased. Now, tell me all that's been going on in your life since I last saw you.'

The time passed pleasantly as Sophie filled Rose in, carefully glossing over her reasons for leaving Buckinghamshire and, instead, telling Aunt Rose about the temporary post, teaching English in Hertfordshire, which had recently come to an end.

Aunt Rose, who was a very discreet lady, had been told by Sophie's parents, when they'd visited, about the way Sophie had been treated by her ex-boyfriend.

'We wish Sophie would talk about it, get it out of her system, but I'm afraid

11

she just clams up if we attempt to raise the subject,' Anne Burnett had said worriedly.

Rose knew from experience that time was a great healer and hoped that, eventually, Sophie would feel able to confide in her.

'Well, what shall we have for supper?' Aunt Rose asked. 'Mavis Briggs has made me a rather nice beef casserole so, if you'd like that it's only a question of heating it up and doing a few additional vegetables.'

'That sounds wonderful,' Sophie assured her. 'Tell me where the vegetables are and I'll prepare them.'

\* \* \*

Over at Rowanbank, Keir sat in Hugh Mercer's comfortable old armchair in the study and thought about Sophie Burnett. She was quite an ordinary-looking girl with an oval face and a quantity of light-brown hair casually tied back, but it was her eyes that had caught his attention. She had the most beautiful eyes, clear grey and long-lashed.

There was obviously a reason why she was free to come to Penbridge in January. He found himself wondering what it was and realised it was the first time he'd shown an interest in any woman since Nina.

Now he came to think of it, Hugh had mentioned a cousin living in Hertfordshire. Keir had a feeling he might have seen Sophie's parents at Hugh's funeral. They had been sitting with Rose Harding. Erica hadn't introduced them to him, but it had been a difficult day for her and she'd had a lot on her mind.

Erica had told Keir about the two mysterious letters that had been left with the will that no-one could make any sense of. He knew one had been for Rose, but Erica hadn't said anything about the recipient of the second one. He made a mental note to ask her.

He smiled and turned his attention to

the sheaf of papers in his hand. He'd no doubt find out more about Sophie Burnett in due course, but for the moment, there were assignments to mark.

\* \* \*

'Are you still selling the dolls' house furniture in the gift shop?' Sophie asked Aunt Rose over supper.

Aunt Rose nodded. 'Most weeks I do a stint behind the counter too — on a voluntary basis. It keeps me occupied and takes me out of the house. I'm not sure if I'd like to work in a charity shop, so this is just right for me. You'd be surprised how many grown-ups love dolls' houses, quite apart from the children.'

'I remember when I was a little girl and we came to stay at Rowanbank one summer. Aunt Mary brought me round to have tea with you and Uncle Tom. You showed me the furniture then and I was absolutely fascinated. Actually, I've still got one or two pieces on the shelf in my bedroom at home now.'

'Have you really, dear? That must have been a few years ago now.'

'It certainly was — I'm thirty-two now!'

'And I'm well in my seventies so, to me, you're just a mere child!'

Sophie laughed and found herself wondering exactly how old Keir was. Nearer forty than thirty, she would have thought.

After they'd finished supper and Sophie had cleared the dishes away, they went into the sitting room to watch TV, but the reception was very poor due to the weather conditions, so they played a game of Scrabble instead. Sophie realised that Aunt Rose was quite an accomplished player.

'Tom loved his game of Scrabble and Hugh and Mary too. We had some good times the four of us. And then, when our partners died within such a very short time of each other, Hugh and I continued to spend some evenings

15

together until he remarried.'

Aunt Rose suddenly looked sad. 'Sometimes Keir pops round and we have a game or two. It's hard to remember he's only been here such a short while.'

'So what does he do? You mentioned an evening class.'

'He's a teacher, like yourself, works part-time in the local senior school, besides taking the classes in the evening. He's a very talented potter and devotes the rest of his time to his own projects. He sells his stuff in the gift shop too. That reminds me he's promised to take some of my dolls' house furniture next time he's passing. I don't expect the shop will be open today in this bad weather.'

★   ★   ★

Sophie lay awake for a while, surprised at the sudden turn of events that had brought her to Kent. She wasn't clear how long she'd stay, but supposed it would be for at least a couple of weeks.

She had thought that the months she'd spent in Hertfordshire, staying with her parents, would have healed her aching heart, but she still missed Brett so very much. She'd met him on a course and they'd discovered they were living and teaching in the same area. Before long they were in a relationship and Sophie was blissfully happy and contemplating a rosy future.

And then the previous Easter, Brett had told her he'd arranged to have a reunion for a few days with some pals from his university days. She said she'd understood and they'd have plenty of time to be together afterwards.

Sophie had been stunned when she'd discovered Brett had been deceiving her and that he'd actually spent the time with a former girlfriend.

'I'm sorry, Sophie,' he'd told her. 'We've had some good times together, but now I'm back with Laura.'

Somehow Sophie managed to get through the next few weeks at school, but then she'd handed in her notice and left at the end of term. Returning to live with her parents in Hertfordshire, she'd enlisted with a teaching agency.

Sophie had been on automatic pilot since then. She supposed she'd have to get round to thinking what she wanted to do with the rest of her life before long. Perhaps coming to Penbridge was a fortuitous interlude. She suspected her mother would have filled Aunt Rose in with the bare outline of what had happened.

As Sophie plumped up her pillows, her thoughts turned to Rowanbank and its new occupant, Keir Ellison. It was good for Aunt Rose to know that there was someone living there at last. It was a big house for one person to live in, but there'd been no mention of a wife or partner. A good-looking man like Keir Ellison was bound to have someone in his life, wasn't he? Not that it was of the slightest interest to Sophie.

The next thing Sophie knew it was morning and it seemed very bright in the room. She checked her watch. It was barely seven o'clock. She realised it must be the snow that made it seem so light. Shrugging on her dressing-gown, she crossed to the window and flung back the curtains. All she could see was a blanket of white. She showered and dressed then sped downstairs.

Ten minutes later she had made the tea and fed the cat, who had eyed her warily and then shot out of the cat flap. Aunt Rose hobbled into the kitchen in her dressing-gown.

'Hello, dear, did you sleep well? It doesn't look any better out there, does it?'

'No, but at least it's stopped snowing.'

As they sat over cups of tea, Sophie made a list of things she could do. It seemed as if they would be snowed in for a few days yet.

'Well, there's no rush,' Aunt Rose said, as they ate breakfast round the kitchen table in comfort. 'I just hope you're not going to be too bored, dear.

You must be used to a busy life.'

'Oh, I'm sure I'll find plenty to do here,' Sophie assured her.

She had been throwing herself into her work to keep herself occupied and had socialised very little since she and Brett had split up. She didn't want time to think.

As if aware of what was going through Sophie's mind, Aunt Rose said, 'Once we've sorted out dinner, I think I'll finish off one or two pieces of dolls' house furniture. Who knows, you might like to help me.'

It wasn't quite what Sophie had in mind, but she was prepared to give it a go. Despite Aunt Rose's protests, after Sophie had finished clearing up in the kitchen and making the beds, she dusted round.

'Now I'm here Mrs Briggs will expect to be back at Rowanbank and anyway, I doubt if she'll be able to get here for a day or two.'

'Oh, I don't like the thought of you doing all this, but it's lovely having a young face around the place. Now, I think we'd better have those lamb chops for lunch — is that OK with you?'

They discussed the rest of the menu and then Sophie peeled the potatoes and prepared the carrots. She wasn't heavily into cooking, but didn't mind helping out. Her mother had sent her with a cherry cake and a bacon joint, along with a several other provisions.

'So thoughtful, but then Anne always was a caring person and it's obvious you take after her, dear,' Rose commented.

Sophie coloured. 'I'm afraid I'm not such a good cook as my mother, but I have looked after myself for a few years. Anyway, just you let me know what needs doing. You must rest that ankle as much as possible and, now that I'm here, you can do just that.'

'Oh, but I need to keep myself active or I'll get stiff. Arthritis, you know. Anyway, you've made a good job of tidying the kitchen and my room so, if you care to get me the box from the cupboard under the stairs I'll make a start on the furniture.'

Sophie found the required box and all the other items that Aunt Rose needed for her morning's work. Aunt Rose reached for her spectacles.

Sophie perched on the edge of a kitchen stool and gazed transfixed at the array of miniature furniture Aunt Rose placed on the table. Besides tiny tables and chairs, there were Welsh dressers and bookcases and even a grand piano.

'Do you make them all yourself, Aunt Rose?'

Rose shook her head. 'It was Tom who used to be so clever at fashioning and staining them. Patience of a saint he had. Nowadays, I buy in kits, but I add individual touches — quilts, curtains, tiny cushions — all those are made by my fair hands. Sometimes I make a batch of dolls as well. I still get orders from time to time, you see.'

Sophie was fascinated, just as she had

been when she'd been a child and Rose's husband, Tom, had allowed her into his workshop. He had been a carpenter by trade and had produced the furniture as a side-line. It had been Rose's brainchild.

Much as Sophie would have loved to linger, she made her excuses and went upstairs to tidy her own room and clean the bathroom.

When she came down again, Keir was sitting at the kitchen table helping Aunt Rose to pack some of the tiny items of dolls' house furniture in tissue paper.

'We wondered where you were — good job the back door was on the latch or Rose would have had to get up to let me in.'

Sophie, normally an even tempered person, bit back a sharp retort.

Rose smiled at her, oblivious of any tension. 'Why don't you put the kettle on, Sophie? We can have an early elevenses.'

All the time Sophie assembled the

coffee things on a tea tray and fetched the biscuit tin, she was aware of Keir's presence. He seemed to have a great deal of patience with Aunt Rose, taking enormous care of the miniature furniture. Sophie wanted to giggle as she heard him exclaim, 'My goodness that's the most perfect example of a Regency chair I've seen for a long time. Anyone would be proud to own that.'

Aunt Rose chuckled. 'My fingers are not quite so nimble as they used to be, I'm afraid, but I still love doing all this. It keeps me occupied. I miss Tom, and Hugh and Mary so much.'

'What about your neighbours in the next cottage? What happened to Mr and Mrs Herbert?' Sophie asked, as she placed the tray carefully on the table.

'Oh, they moved away to be nearer their daughter and grandchildren. They've got a lovely bungalow in Eastbourne. They sent me some photographs with their Christmas card. You should see their garden. It's an absolute picture, although I expect it's under snow like here at the moment. They've invited me to stay, but I don't know if I will. Sometimes things seem a bit of an effort these days, you know.'

Keir moved the dolls' house furniture out of range of the coffee cups.

'So who lives in Laburnum Cottage now?' Sophie persisted.

'Oh, a young couple who work in London during the week. I hardly ever see them, but they're pleasant enough. They were away all over Christmas and New Year too.'

'Fiona and Ian Knight,' Keir supplied. 'I've seen them around the village from time to time at the weekends.'

'Didn't Dad tell me that you and your family used to live in Laburnum Cottage at one time, Aunt Rose?'

'That's right. I was brought up there and Tom was brought up here. When I got married I moved into this cottage. Tom said it was intended with it being called Rose Cottage. By then, Mary was already married to Hugh and living in Rowanbank. Eventually, when Hugh's parents died he inherited the house.'

Keir looked thoughtful. I'd no idea you'd lived in Laburnum Cottage, Rose. How interesting.'

'Well, this was a close knit community once upon a time. It's a pity things have to change, but there it is. We've got a lot of incomers nowadays.'

'Myself included, eh?' He laughed at the look of horror on Rose's face, as she realised what she'd said. 'Don't worry, Rose. I know exactly what you meant, but how long does it take before I stop being an incomer, I wonder?' he added teasingly.

Poppy suddenly appeared through the cat flap and to Sophie's surprise made a beeline for Keir who tickled her under the chin with his free hand.

'Hello, old girl. So what do you make of all this white stuff then?'

Much to Sophie's amusement, Poppy meowed.

'She definitely doesn't like it,' Keir decided. 'Oh, well, I suppose I'd better be on my way. Schools closed due to the heating breaking down, but I've got plenty to be getting on with in the way of paperwork.'

'Sophie's a teacher too,' Aunt Rose informed him.

His expressive eyes surveyed Sophie intently. 'Really, there's a lot of us about. So I take it you're in between jobs, being as it's term-time.'

Sophie nodded, hoping he wasn't about to ask her any awkward questions.

'I'm registered with an agency, but I've decided to have a few weeks off in between posts.'

'Good idea Everyone needs a sabbatical. We must have a chat sometime. Now, if you'll excuse me. If there's anything you need, Rose, give me a shout . . . By the way, I've put a tarpaulin over your car, Sophie.'

Sophie murmured her thanks.

Padding across the floor in his thick socks, he stood by the back door and pulled on his Wellingtons and then realised he'd left the dolls' house furniture on the table.

Sophie picked up the box and handed it to him, catching her breath as her fingers brushed his and she again experienced a tingling sensation, sending a little shiver along her spine.

'Stay in the warm,' he advised her, hand on the door latch and, a moment later, he was gone.

Aunt Rose smiled. 'He's such a delightful young man. I'm so pleased he's moved in to Rowanbank.'

Sophie was suddenly curious to know more about him.

'Does he live there on his own?'

'Well, so far as I'm aware, there's no wife or partner living at Rowanbank, but I don't stand at the window and monitor his comings and goings,' the older woman chided gently.

Sophie busied herself at the sink, washing up the coffee cups. It was obvious she wasn't going to learn much from Aunt Rose.

'I'm just glad Keir's taking an interest in putting Rowanbank to rights.

The garden was in a bit of a mess, although Erica did get someone in to mow the lawns and tidy it up periodically.'

'Do you ever hear from Erica?' Sophie asked, thinking of Uncle Hugh's young widow, as she dried the cups.

'No, not even a Christmas card. Of course, Erica and I didn't exactly see eye to eye on one or two things. Actually, I did hear she'd gone to Spain to stay with friends. She's welcome. I wouldn't like the climate or the food!'

Sophie had only met Erica on a couple of occasions, but from what she had gathered, knew her to be a rather hard, ruthless sort of individual. She had cleared Rowanbank of virtually every memory of Aunt Mary, and had made it clear that Aunt Rose was no longer welcome to call, except by invitation. According to Sophie's parents, Erica had barely spoken to Aunt Rose on the day of Hugh's funeral.

After lunch, Sophie settled down to helping Aunt Rose with the tiny quilt and pillows for the dolls' house beds. She found it surprisingly satisfying and therapeutic.

'All we need now is a small girl to play with them,' Sophie said, studying their handiwork with a sense of pleasure.

'Yes, that was my one sadness, not having any children, but when my niece, Daphne, comes, she'll bring her little girl. Do you remember the dolls' house Uncle Tom made for you when you were knee-high to a grasshopper?'

'Of course, I do! It was one of my treasured possessions for years and the envy of my schoolfriends. We gave it to the vicar's children a few years back.'

'It's nice to know it went to a good home. Time for a cuppa I reckon — no let me. I'm not an invalid and, hopefully, my ankle will soon be fine.'

'Do you have to go back to the hospital?'

Aunt Rose shook her head. 'I've just to see the nurse, if this weather ever bucks up sufficiently for me to get to the surgery.'

'Oh, it will and I'll take you,' Sophie said, thinking how pleased she'd be to take a look round the village when they could get out.

Living at Rose Cottage seemed as if it was going to be one perpetual round of coffee and tea, Sophie thought. But, she had to admit, that she'd enjoyed the relaxing afternoon.

Perhaps it was what she needed. Time out to reflect on what to do next with her life.

# A Mysterious Letter

It was several days more before the weather showed any sign of improvement and then there was a sudden thaw and the snow turned into slush. Eventually, after a night of rain, Sophie was able to don her Wellingtons and anorak and set off for the village. Aunt Rose told her to take her time and that she'd be perfectly all right until lunchtime.

She was struggling with the tarpaulin on the car when Keir Ellison appeared.

'Hi, I was intending to give you a ring. If you're going into the village I could give you a lift in the Range Rover.'

She hesitated fractionally and then took up his offer and scrambled in beside him.

'So you're not at work today then?'

'No, it's my day off. I've got one or

two things to do in the village and then I'm spending the afternoon working on my ceramics. I suppose I ought to call into the gift shop to check whether I've had any sales.'

'You don't sound very hopeful.'

He shrugged. 'Firstly, it's the wrong time of the year and, secondly, the gift shop is looking tired these days and doesn't attract many customers. Of course, Peggy Munn, who runs it, must be over eighty. I can't imagine how the place pays.'

'Are you telling me, Mrs Munn still works there? Her late husband, Ron, was a great friend of my Uncle Hugh's.'

'Yes, I've gathered Ron was quite a character. Look, why don't you come with me? Then you can find out if Rose has sold anything.'

'OK, just to say hello. I've got a list of things to do, and I've promised to be back around lunch time, although it's all prepared.'

★ ★ ★

Peggy Munn's face creased into a smile as they entered the shop.

'Well, what a surprise! It's Sophie Burnett, isn't it? Rose told me on the phone you were staying with her. It's lovely to see you again — and Mr Ellison too. So what can I do for the pair of you?'

Sophie crossed to the counter and took Peggy's gnarled hand.

'Oh, I've just called in to say, hello, and to see if there've been any sales for Aunt Rose recently.'

'Likewise, for myself,' Keir added, 'although I should think it's highly improbable with all this bad weather.'

Peggy bent down and took a couple of worn notebooks from a shelf under the counter. She thumbed through the top one and shook her head, white curls bobbing, and then picked up the second.

'I'm sorry, but there's been nothing since the middle of last week, unless — wait a minute, I seem to remember . . . '

Peggy disappeared beneath the counter again, and Sophie and Keir exchanged amused glances. This time she emerged holding some dog-eared scraps of paper.

'My son stood in for me for a couple of hours and wrote everything on here.'

They waited patiently as she scrutinised the writing. 'Oh my goodness. He's got such appalling handwriting!'

She passed the paper across to Keir and together he and Sophie managed to decipher the scrawl, deciding that Keir had sold a vase and two pendants whilst Aunt Rose had sold three sets of dolls' house furniture.

Another customer entered the shop just then and Sophie took the opportunity to take a look round. It was like an Aladdin's cave, she decided, brimming with knick-knacks ranging from tiny pottery animals, to select pieces of china and glass for the more discerning eye. There was, however, a slight air of neglect these days. Sophie supposed the elderly lady couldn't keep abreast of all that was needed.

Keir's ceramics and Aunt Rose's dolls' house furniture were displayed in a glass cabinet. Sophie loved the vibrant colours of Keir's work — rich purple and turquoise, apple green and cerise.

As they left the shop, Sophie carefully stowed the envelope containing Aunt Rose's cash in her handbag and Keir placed his in his wallet.

'There's something I'd like to run past you. I could do with a coffee and I'm sure you could too, so shall we meet back here in around twenty minutes?'

Sophie agreed, feeling a little thrill of pleasure that he'd asked her to join him, but wondering what on earth he could want to discuss with her.

Having completed her tasks, she arrived back at the gift shop just as Keir came round the corner. Taking her arm, he steered her into a small cafe which was at the side of a bakers. It was warm and welcoming and there was a wonderful aroma of spicy buns and newly baked bread.

'Sit yourself down. I'll get these,' he told her, and she found a corner table and looked about her at the bright walls adorned with flower prints and the oak beams and the original fireplace which now sported a gas fire with leaping flames. She didn't remember there being a teashop here before.

Sophie watched Keir as he stood chatting for a moment to the girl at the counter thinking again what an attractive man he was. He'd got a charming personality too and obviously fitted well into the village community.

He'd certainly won Aunt Rose's vote and it was comforting to know that she had such a caring neighbour living nearby.

Keir came across with the coffee and a couple of the spicy buns. She reached for her purse, but he waived the offer aside.

'No, this is on me. As I've said, I want to sound you out about something.'

'What's that?' she asked curiously,

reaching for a napkin.

'What do you make of the gift shop?'

She wrinkled her brow. 'How do you mean — what do I make of it? It's roughly the same as it's always been — perhaps a little more cluttered and a little dustier.'

He nodded. 'Exactly what other people have said. Don't you think it could do with a bit of a makeover?'

Sophie frowned. 'But then it wouldn't be the same, would it? And that's what people like — continuity. Anyway, I'm not sure if Peggy Munn could afford it.'

'Mmm, but at the moment it seems more like the old curiosity shop — some of that stuff must have been knocking around for decades.'

'But if that's what keeps Mrs Munn busy and happy, why should it matter to us?' Sophie asked sharply.

'That's not really any way to run a business, is it?' he chided gently.

'Oh, I see, you're thinking of how it affects you and your work, is that it?'

He met her grey eyes steadily with his

own brown ones — the colour of sherry, she decided again.

'Well, obviously I've got a vested interest and so has Rose, together with a few other people in the area. Fortunately, the gift shop's not my only outlet, but if it were, I'd be very concerned.'

'But if Mrs Munn is good enough to display your goods then surely you shouldn't complain,' she said feeling a little prickle of anger rising in her as she sprang to the defence of the elderly lady.

Keir had the grace to bow his head, but not before she'd seen the twinkle in his eyes.

'Have I said something amusing?' she demanded, stirring her coffee vigorously.

'Well, no it's just that you sound a little like the head of department at the school where I work. Seriously though, Sophie, we are in the twenty-first century, so we've got to move with the times.'

Her cheeks turned pink. 'If you say so. Well, you know what, Keir? You could always take your stuff out of the shop, if it doesn't suit you, and display it somewhere else.'

Much to Sophie's surprise, he meekly agreed with her. 'It might come to that, but I like Mrs Munn and she doesn't ask for too much commission. I suspect she waives it all together for Rose.'

'Actually, Aunt Rose sometimes helps out in the shop on a voluntary basis, but, anyway, I doubt if her dolls' house furniture sells for the sort of prices your ceramics do,' Sophie pointed out.

'True,' he conceded and put a hand over hers. The contact was electric, sending a little shiver quivering along her spine. This man was seriously attractive, but she wasn't looking for a romantic entanglement so soon after parting from Brett.

Anyway, a man with Keir's charm and looks must surely be involved with someone already. She pulled herself together with an effort.

'I like your pottery,' she told him sincerely. 'The colours are wonderful.'

'Thank you — are you into ceramics?' he asked with interest.

'I don't know much about making pottery, but I do appreciate it. I certainly know what I like when I see it,' she said. 'My father took me to exhibitions and galleries from quite an early age.'

Keir told her about a recent exhibition he'd been to in London. He was an interesting man to talk to and Sophie felt herself relaxing in his company. The time passed pleasantly until, suddenly catching sight of the clock above the counter, she shot to her feet.

'Thanks so much for coffee, but I've got a couple more things to do now and Aunt Rose will wonder where I've got to.'

★　★　★

'Well, you two look as if you've had a busy morning,' Aunt Rose told them, as

41

they entered the kitchen.

'Sorry if we're a bit late, Rose,' Keir said setting down the shopping bag he was carrying. 'It was easier to take the Range Rover and I have to confess we sneaked into the cafe for a coffee.'

Aunt Rose's eyes twinkled. 'Did you now? Then it's just as well I wasn't waiting for those groceries, wasn't it? Actually, I've had a visitor whilst you've been out. Mavis Briggs popped by to see how I was getting along. She says it's like a palace upstairs, thanks to you, Sophie. You obviously take after your mother for keeping things spick and span. Anyway, she made me a cuppa and we've had a good long natter setting the country to rights as usual.'

Keir stayed just long enough to fill Rose in with what was happening at the gift shop, refused lunch graciously and left.

'I take it you two are getting along all right then?' Aunt Rose said casually.

'Oh, Keir's very pleasant company.'

Sophie thought she detected a gleam in Aunt Rose's eyes and hoped she was mistaken. Sophie wasn't ready for a new relationship yet. She was still recovering from Brett and feeling emotionally bruised. But, she had to admit Keir was a very attractive man and it would be good to have him as a friend with no strings attached.

Sophie wondered if she ought to make any comment about the gift shop, but decided to be cautious. She handed Aunt Rose the envelope containing her earnings.

Aunt Rose looked inside and sighed. 'Thank you, dear. I'm afraid there's not much left over these days after I've covered the cost of the materials, but after all, I suppose it is only a hobby, and it's better than me sitting twiddling my thumbs, isn't it? Now, Mavis Briggs has put that meat pie in the oven for me, so if you could just pop the veg on we can still eat fairly early. What's it like out?'

'Cold, but crisp underfoot. There's

still a bit of ice and snow around.'

Sophie busied herself at the cooker and then put the shopping away under Aunt Rose's directions.

'I've had a bit of a body blow,' the old lady said quietly. 'I know I ought to have seen it coming, but I've been shutting my mind to it, hoping it wouldn't happen any time soon.'

Sophie spun round from the cooker. 'Whatever's happened, Aunt Rose? Are you ill?' she asked in alarm.

'No, dear, it's nothing like that. I probably haven't told you about the plans for the disused chapel just off the high street?'

Sophie wrinkled her brow. 'I don't think so.'

'No, well, I suppose I've been burying my head in the sand, hoping it might all come to nothing. Anyway, it seems they're forging ahead with converting it into a craft centre. There have been ongoing discussions about what to do with the building since way before Hugh died. It's been quite controversial and thrown up a number of issues, such as whether it's right to use a chapel for that sort of project.'

'Really. I'm surprised Keir didn't mention it.' Sophie said, taken aback.

'Perhaps he didn't like to. After all, he must realise how strongly some of us older folk feel about it. Of course, looking at it from Keir's point of view, I can quite see that it might be a better outlet for his wares, and he'd have space to work there too. It's understandable that the incomers can't have the same feelings for Peggy Munn's as those of us who've lived in Penbridge all our lives.'

Sophie felt indignant on Aunt Rose's behalf. She wondered if Keir had been sounding her out before telling her about the craft centre. Sophie had made her feelings plain when he'd mentioned the shortcomings of the gift shop and so that was probably why he hadn't filled her in.

He'd probably been getting round to it and changed his mind, realising he wasn't likely to get Sophie on his side over this.

'There's been a great deal of discussion and some opposition,' Aunt Rose continued. 'Some people wanted the old chapel to be used for a restaurant or a more permanent home for the farmers' market. Someone even suggested turning it into a small heritage centre, but the craft centre was top of the list.

'It had all gone quiet recently, so Mavis and I hoped it might have been shelved, but I suppose things have just been at a bit of a stand-still over Christmas and New Year. Anyway, now it seems there's a grant available to say nothing of a substantial donation from an anonymous benefactor, so it's all going to happen — more's the pity!'

Seeing Aunt Rose was visibly upset, Sophie checked the vegetables and came to sit beside her for a moment and tried to comfort her.

'Of course, it will probably finish Peggy Munn's business if this craft centre takes off, and I couldn't afford to put my stuff anywhere else. Besides, Peggy and I have built up a good relationship over the years.'

Sophie patted Rose's hand. 'Oh, but surely it won't come to that, I mean folk know what they like and Mrs Munn's shop has been going for donkey's years.'

'That's the problem,' Aunt Rose said gloomily. 'It's all change these days. Peggy owns the building that the shop's in, and I can't see her giving up without a struggle, but it'll have a knock-on effect with the likes of myself — you mark my words.'

Sophie sympathised with the elderly lady, realising she was probably right.

Aunt Rose opened the cutlery drawer and began to set the table. 'Although my dolls' house furniture doesn't pay much, as I've told you, it does help out with the bills. I've got to have some decorating done this year. I like to keep this place looking nice and then there's a fence to replace. These things don't come cheap. Actually Sophie, I had been promised a little something from Hugh's estate when he died, but it didn't come to fruition. You see there was this rather curious letter left for me with Hugh's will.'

Sophie nodded. 'My parents received one too and well, like you've said, nothing came of it.'

'Yes, Hugh was very fond of your parents and I felt sure he would have remembered them in some way. Of course, once Erica came on the scene things radically changed, but, judging from the date, those letters were written long before then. Whoever would have thought he would have married again at his age and someone young enough to be his daughter!'

'I suppose she's quite a wealthy woman now,' Sophie said carefully, picking up the vibes. It was evident that there was no love lost between Aunt Rose and Erica.

Aunt Rose sniffed. 'If that's a polite way of saying she's the merry widow, well yes, she is. Hugh was heavily involved in charitable work and was always very generous, but Erica could twist him round her little finger, and I know he would have provided well for her. Let's have our lunch now before it's ruined and afterwards you can take a look at that letter I received from Hugh's solicitor.'

★   ★   ★

Aunt Rose hunted in her workbox, brought out a letter and handed it to Sophie.

'Are you sure you want me to read this?'

Aunt Rose nodded and Sophie removed the sheet of paper from the envelope. It was roughly the same letter as the one her parents had received and equally as puzzling.

*Dear Rose,*
*You will find I've already remem-bered you and left you something of*

*value, but you will need to think about this very carefully.*

*Much love,*
*Hugh*

Rose frowned. 'I'm wondering if Hugh wasn't quite himself when he wrote that. Whatever can it mean?'

Sophie shook her head. 'My parents are as mystified as you are, and think pretty much the same thing. They've had gifts from Hugh over the years, but nothing that was particularly valuable. It's all a bit of a mystery, isn't it?'

Rose turned her head away and there was a catch in her voice when she spoke.

'Of course, none of us expected Hugh to die so suddenly. He'd been in good health or so we thought, and then he had that massive heart attack. I suppose there's a possibility he hadn't got round to giving us those gifts, whatever they were. Oh, well, I suppose we'll never know now,' she said wistfully.

# An Invitation

A couple of days later Sophie was able to take Aunt Rose to see the nurse. After the pace of working in a town, Penbridge appeared amazingly sleepy. It seemed that Rose knew several people in the surgery and assured Sophie she'd be fine if Sophie would like to go off and collect the library books that had been reserved for her.

Reaching the end of the road, Sophie decided she must have taken a wrong turning. She was hesitating when someone tapped her on the shoulder.

Startled, she spun round to find Keir smiling down at her. 'Off on more errands?'

'I'm supposed to be going to the library whilst Aunt Rose is at the surgery seeing the nurse, but I appear to be lost,' she admitted, feeling ridiculously pleased to see him.

'Well, you're getting warm. If you backtrack and take the turning on your right, you'll come straight to it. Tell you what, why don't I come with you? It's not too much out of my way.'

'Oh, there's no need,' she assured him, but he ignored this and set off at such a pace that she had difficulty keeping up with him. 'Could you slow down a bit?' she asked, breathlessly. 'We're not in for a race.'

He grinned and took her arm casually. 'Sorry I forgot you're a city girl and I take walloping big strides. How long are you planning to stay with Rose?'

'I've no idea,' she assured him truthfully.

He gave her a searching look from those brown eyes, so that she wanted to turn away from his scrutiny, wondering what he was thinking. She was tempted to ask Keir what had brought him to Penbridge but suspected he wouldn't be forthcoming.

'Well, I must press on — can you find

your own way back?'

She nodded, but found herself wishing he would stay. She had to admit she enjoyed his company.

It was warm inside the library and there was a friendly atmosphere. Everyone appeared to know everyone else. The librarian, chirpy and blonde, looked at her with a smile of recognition. 'Sophie Burnett! Long time no see!'

Sophie beamed at Mavis Briggs' daughter. 'Crystal! I'd forgotten you worked here.'

'My mum told me you were staying with Mrs Harding. Have you come to collect her books? I was so sorry to learn she'd had an accident. Such a pity she's not nearer the village. It's good to know her neighbour's been keeping an eye on her, though. Mr Ellison's such a nice man.'

Crystal paused to scan an elderly couple's books and to pass the time of day with them.

'We had some great times years back

at Rowanbank, didn't we?' Sophie said. 'How's your sister?'

Crystal reached for Rose's books and took the library card Sophie handed her.

'Oh, Teresa's fine. Her little girl's almost eight now. Amy loves to visit Mrs Harding to see the dolls' house furniture, just as we did when we were children.'

The rather plump lady, who was next in the queue, was looking impatient and Crystal said hastily, 'Won't be a minute, Mrs Thomas. Look, I'd love to catch up some time, Sophie.' She scrawled her phone number on a card and popped it inside the top book.

Leaving the library, Sophie saw Keir was still standing outside. He was deep in conversation with a stylish, auburn-haired young woman. Her hand was on Keir's sleeve and she was hanging on to his every word.

Sophie paused and, a few moments later, the red-head made off in the direction of an alleyway between two houses. Distracted, Sophie continued down the steps and missed her footing on the last one, scattering books in all directions.

The next moment, she found herself enfolded in a pair of strong arms, her head leaning against a broad, muscular chest.

'Are you OK?' enquired Keir, solicitously.

'Thank you, yes,' she mumbled into his coat. She straightened up, feeling unspeakably foolish but, at the same time, aware of just how comforting it felt to be held so close by such a deeply attractive man.

Keir did not immediately release her and she could feel her heart beating a wild tattoo.

'Are you quite sure you're OK?' he asked again gently. 'I mean, we don't want two casualties in the cottage, do we now?'

'I'm fine,' she assured him, enjoying being in the shelter of his arms for a moment longer. 'Why don't you catch up with your friend.'

'Oh, Glenda's one of my students. I run a couple of ceramics classes in the evenings at the school where I work.'

He gathered up the library books and handed them to her, looking rather amused.

'Well, if you're quite sure you're in one piece, at least let me give you this.'

He produced a folded shopping bag from his capacious pocket and held it open for her, as she popped the books in. He was obviously one of those infuriatingly, organised people who was always ready for every emergency.

She thanked him again and walked off with as much dignity as she could muster, aware that at least two ladies from the library were watching her curiously from their stand by the window, and that Aunt Rose would be champing at the bit by now.

Crystal Briggs phoned Sophie that evening to invite her over to her home for coffee the following evening, as her parents were going out for a meal. Now that the snow had gone, Aunt Rose was feeling a lot happier and had arranged for one of her friends from the WI to pop in and keep her company.

Crystal and Sophie had always got on well and the more they chatted, the more they recalled happy summers when the sun had always shone and they'd gone off for cycle rides.

'Those halcyon days can't be recaptured — more's the pity,' Crystal sighed. 'Everything's changing and not necessarily for the better. I keep wondering how long it'll be before they talk about closing the library.'

'Oh, surely not! It seemed pretty full when I went in the other day.'

Crystal sighed. 'Yes, but that's not significant. It's a small concern and the building's ancient. I can see us having to amalgamate with one of the larger ones and then we'll all have to reapply for our jobs and everyone in the village will have to rely on a mobile library van.'

Sophie sympathised. It seemed an ideal moment to mention the rumours concerning the new craft centre. Crystal nodded.

'That's a classic example of what I'm talking about. I suppose I can see the benefit for certain people. You ought to have been at some of those meetings. I take it you've actually met Keir Ellison from Rowanbank?'

Sophie grinned. 'On more than one occasion.' She filled her in with their last meeting outside the library and Crystal burst out laughing.

'Wished I'd seen that! Lucky you falling into his arms! He's good-looking, isn't he? You're blushing!'

Sophie lowered her gaze, annoyed with herself for displaying her feelings.

'Go on — what were you going to say about Keir?'

'Well, for a incomer he was quite vocal at the meetings. Upset some of the older residents who'd lived here all their lives and wanted very different things for the village.'

'I see — was Aunt Rose there?' she asked.

'No, but Fiona and Ian Knight, her neighbours from Laburnum Cottage, were and they were fully in support of Keir, as were many of the younger generation. And then there was a contingent representing the opposing view, including Peggy Munn's son. Yes, there were some lively discussions during those meetings.'

'So what would you like to see happening?' asked Sophie.

'To be honest, I quite like the idea of a craft centre, but perhaps it's a bit ambitious. My parents were in favour of the old chapel being used as a new venue for the farmers' market. At the moment it's held in the village hall, but that's not always available or so central. Anyway, it looks as if the craft centre's going ahead so everyone will just have to get used to it whether they like it, or not — more coffee?'

'Please. I'm concerned about the impact this will have on Aunt Rose and

Peggy Munn's business,' Sophie said worriedly.

Crystal poured the coffee. 'Let's be brutally honest, Sophie, that gift shop is sadly in need of a makeover. I think it's a great place, don't get me wrong, but some of the stock must have been there for decades, like poor old Peggy.'

'But, it would break her heart if she was drummed out of business by this new craft centre and I don't suppose she can afford any improvements to the shop.'

As they sat over second cups of coffee and slabs of Mrs Briggs' fruit cake Crystal asked, as Sophie had know she would, 'So what's been going on in your life recently? How come you've got the time to come here in January? Sorry, was it a relationship?' she prompted, seeing the bleak expression in Sophie's eyes.

Sophie nodded. 'It didn't work out — end of story,' she murmured, not wanting to enlarge on what had happened. 'I suppose I must be one of the most gullible women in the universe. I didn't see it coming.'

'Men, eh? So do I take it that's why you left your permanent job in Bucks?'

'Yes, I returned to live with my parents for a few months.'

Sophie told Crystal briefly about the agency work.

'I've no idea how long Rose needs me here, but it makes a pleasant change from town life. So what about you?'

Crystal shrugged. 'Oh, I was going out with someone for a time, but then he moved away because of his work. We kept in touch but, after a bit, things fizzled out. Sad, isn't it? I keep thinking some gorgeous hunk of a man will walk into the library one day and sweep me off my feet!'

Sophie smiled as she had a flashback of Keir rescuing her from outside the library and remembered the warmth of his arms about her. She shrugged off the memory. She'd got absolutely no intention of getting romantically involved with Keir Ellison. For one thing she was only staying in Penbridge for a week or two and, for another, she'd just learnt he was involved in an enterprise that was inevitably going to have such a devastating effect on Aunt Rose and Peggy Munn.

Crystal told her that, although Keir was throwing himself wholeheartedly into village life, no-one seemed to know too much about his background.

'He seems to be a bit of a mystery man. He's passionate about his ceramics, that I do know, and it's infectious. He runs a couple of evening classes at the secondary school where he works. They've got kilns, and I've had to order in a load of books on ceramics from other libraries.'

Crystal passed her the plate of chocolate biscuits and they nibbled in silence for a moment or two.

'Changing the subject, has anyone mentioned the concert on Saturday?'

Sophie shook her head. 'Tell me more.'

'It's a police concert, brass band, to

raise money for the church roof appeal and some other charity, which slips my mind for the minute. Anyway, I've got a couple of tickets if you'd care to come. The friend I was going with has had to cry off because her youngest has got the dreaded lurgy.'

'Oh, what a shame! I'd feel a bit guilty leaving Aunt Rose, but if she didn't mind, that would be great.'

'There are some rather good looking gentlemen in that band!'

Sophie laughed and realised that, for the first time in ages, she hadn't been spending every waking minute thinking about Brett.

When she mentioned the concert to Aunt Rose the older woman nodded.

'Peggy and I had intended going to that, but we've decided against it. Those seats are so hard and her knee's playing up again. Anyway, you go and enjoy yourself. It's so popular the tickets sell like hotcakes. Perhaps you could drop me off at Peggy's and I could keep her company. A couple of old crocks together!'

Sophie laughed. She was enjoying her time in Penbridge and got on well with Aunt Rose. Nothing had been said about how long she was to stay, and she realised she'd need to broach the subject sooner or later.

Keir appeared at the back door balancing a box of eggs.

'Compliments of the vicar's wife. She sent them via Mavis. Frances didn't realise you'd been in trouble, Rose, what with the snow and everything — said you should have given her a ring.'

Sophie put the kettle on yet again and, presently, they sat round the kitchen table enjoying a fresh brew and some ginger cake that she'd bought at the local bakery.

'I'm actually killing two birds with one stone,' Keir said. 'I was wondering if the pair of you would like to accompany me to the police concert on Saturday?'

Sophie felt a pang of disappointment

and Aunt Rose explained for both of them.

'Right, then would you mind if I accompanied you and Crystal, Sophie?'

'I, erm — that would be nice,' she mumbled, feeling like a schoolgirl being asked out on her first date.

'Have you already got the tickets?' asked Aunt Rose.

'Yes, but that doesn't matter. They're crying out for them so I can sell the spares, if I can't find a home for them. I could even ask one of my students along to make up the party.'

Sophie's heart had been hammering ridiculously, but now she realised he was just being kind. She wasn't sure how Crystal would react to having a student foisted upon her.

Keir set down his cup. 'You must come over to my place for tea some time soon. I'm always accepting your hospitality, Rose.'

Rose shifted uncomfortably in her chair and mumbled something non commital and, shortly afterwards, Keir departed.

'Have you ever been across to Rowanbank since Keir's been living there?' Sophie asked casually.

Aunt Rose was busily examining the eggs. 'Look at those! Still got some feathers sticking to them. That's so kind of Frances. I don't know how she fits everything in. Could you pop them in the larder for me, dear? In answer to your question, no I haven't set foot in Rowanbank since Hugh's funeral. Quite frankly, it distresses me to see what Erica's done to the place. Poor Mary would turn in her grave.'

'Well, I suppose it's inevitable that she'd want to put her own stamp on things, just as Keir will want to do,' Sophie said reasonably.

Rose did not reply to this merely asking, 'Do you fancy macaroni cheese for supper?'

Sophie was dying to see the inside of Rowanbank again and was disappointed that Aunt Rose hadn't accepted Keir's invitation.

On Saturday, Sophie was undecided

what to wear. She hadn't brought much with her, not intending to stay long. In the end, she decided on black trousers teamed with an attractive, coral pink tunic top, which she supposed wouldn't be seen anyway beneath her wool jacket.

Keir turned up promptly at six-fifteen. 'Alan's going straight there because it's first come first serve with the seats. Apparently, only families and special friends have reserved ones in the front rows.'

'And they're welcome, because brass bands can be very noisy,' Aunt Rose pronounced. 'Peggy always removes her hearing aid.'

Sophie met Keir's amused eyes and lowered her gaze, as she felt her lips twitching.

They deposited Rose at Peggy Munn's and arranged to collect her about ten o'clock.

Crystal was talking to some friends just inside the village hall when they arrived.

'So where's this mystery friend of Keir's?' she hissed, as Keir showed the tickets.

'Apparently he's gone ahead to reserve some seats.'

Alan turned out to be a mature student from Keir's evening class, whose daytime job was with computers. Much to Sophie's relief, it wasn't long before Crystal and Alan were chatting animatedly.

The concert was brilliant. Sophie sat enthralled, periodically stealing a glance at Keir who appeared to be equally rapt. At one point, during a particularly uplifting piece, he placed his hand over hers making her pulse race.

During the interval, Sophie went with Keir to get some refreshments, leaving Alan and Crystal engrossed in their conversation.

'So what do you think?'

'About the concert or about Crystal and Alan?' Sophie enquired.

'Both.' They were standing in a queue and, glancing across the hall, Sophie could see Crystal and Alan still deep in conversation.

'They seem to be getting on OK,' she said with a smile. 'Why, do you fancy a new vocation as matchmaker?'

He laughed and, seeing a gap in the queue, caught hold of her arm and moved forward.

Sophie caught her breath, feeling as though she'd received an electric charge. Keir was having a serious effect on her and she'd only known him such a short time. Well, it was no good getting involved. She was only here for another week at the outside. Besides, she was decidedly off men, wasn't she, after Brett? But emotions were stirring inside her which had been dormant during the past months and she was finding it increasingly difficult to ignore them.

'That was delightful,' Keir pronounced, when the concert came to an end shortly before ten o'clock. Everyone agreed.

'Anyone for a drink?' asked Alan.

Sophie and Keir declined on account of picking up Rose from Peggy Munn's. Crystal looked disappointed but brightened when Alan suggested the two of them went anyway.

Sophie caught her friend's eye and winked, and Crystal turned pink.

Sophie and Keir could have walked the short distance to Peggy's and Sophie was disappointed that they'd arrived so quickly. She'd enjoyed the evening and wished it could have gone on longer. She pulled herself together sharply. In all probability, Keir had someone tucked away. Perhaps they were having an amicable separation to give themselves some space.

Aunt Rose didn't seem in any hurry to leave and Peggy insisted on putting the kettle on for more tea. Peggy's sitting room was rather like the gift shop, only not so dusty. It was full to bursting with knick-knacks. A large ginger cat sat and surveyed them warily from his perch on the arm of a chair. Keir carried the tray for Peggy and set it down carefully.

He then handed round cups of rather milky tea, followed by a plate of garibaldi biscuits.

'I was telling Rose how much I missed her in the shop on Thursday,' Peggy said.

'During the winter months I'm only opening between ten and four o'clock, and I'm closed all day on Wednesdays and Saturday afternoons.'

'Well, if I'm free next Thursday, and Aunt Rose doesn't mind, I could come and give you a hand,' Sophie volunteered.

'Would you, dear? That would be such a help. My son, John, and his wife lend a hand when they can, but they don't get much free time. John's not quite retired yet, you see.'

Sophie went into the kitchen to wash the cups and Keir followed.

'Well, we've had that drink, after all. Lovely pair of ladies, aren't they?'

Sophie smilingly agreed. 'I've known them all my life.'

'So do I understand you're planning to be around for a while yet, then?'

'I haven't got the remotest idea,' she told him truthfully.

He leant towards her. 'Only, if you were perhaps . . . '

He trailed off as Peggy Munn came into the kitchen.

'Oh, you shouldn't have troubled to wash up — those pots would have kept til the morning. I've had such a lovely natter to Rose. Thank you so much for bringing her here, Mr Ellison.'

'Keir,' he told her smilingly.

'Your parents must have named you after that Scottish politician — Keir Hardie.'

His eyes danced with amusement. 'That's an interesting thought,' he told her, 'but I think it was more likely to have been after a hero in a book she was reading at the time. Now, I think I'd better run Rose and Sophie home.'

'I'll look forward to seeing you next week, dear,' the old lady told Sophie.

Sophie nodded, wishing that Peggy

hadn't chosen that precise moment to come into the kitchen. What had Keir been about to say?

★  ★  ★

'Well, that was a very pleasant evening,' Aunt Rose said, as they sat over breakfast the following morning. 'I feel quite like my old self.' She glanced at the clock. 'So much so that I'm wondering — how do you feel about accompanying me to church? We've still got enough time.'

'Well, if you're sure you can manage. Isn't there rather a lot of up and downing?'

'Oh, I can just stay seated and it's a family service today, according to the parish magazine, so it'll be fairly short.'

Sophie didn't point out that the pews would surely be equally as hard as the village hall chairs. She hurriedly washed up, helped prepare the vegetables, slammed in the joint and set the automatic timer, before dashing upstairs to change into something more respectable than a pair of jeans and a sweatshirt.

* * *

The service was about to begin when Sophie helped Aunt Rose into a pew. A moment or two later they were joined by Keir. He squeezed in beside Sophie and shared her hymn book, singing lustily in a deep tenor. She was incredibly aware of him and tried hard to concentrate, but was getting wafts of his cologne. As he closed the hymn book his fingers brushed hers, sending a little frisson dancing along her spine.

A shaft of wintry sunlight filtered through the stained glass window of the Norman church streaking Keir's fair hair with gold. Sophie pulled herself together with an effort.

The vicar, a family man with two children of his own, was excellent with the youngsters in the congregation. At the end of the service, he gave out one or two notices.

Looking across at Keir he said, 'Keir Ellison would like me to remind you that he'll be giving a talk on ceramics on Tuesday, in the village hall, at seven-thirty. Tickets on the door to include refreshments, courtesy of our church ladies, and all proceeds to the church roof fund. It's good to know that Keir's as keen to help with charitable works as Hugh Mercer, our last incumbent of Rowanbank was.'

A number of people swivelled round to look in Keir's direction and he smiled. Sophie could see the tips of his ears had turned pink and wondered if he was as confident as he appeared.

'Shall we stay for a coffee?' Aunt Rose asked when the service was over. 'I need to thank Frances for those eggs, and have a word with one or two other people I haven't caught up with recently.'

Keir consulted his watch. 'I'm off out to lunch, but a quick cup would be welcome. It's a chilly old morning.'

'We seem to be making a habit of

this,' Keir said, as he and Sophie juggled with cups of coffee and biscuits.

Sophie laughed. 'Yes, tea and coffee do seem to figure rather a lot when we meet up. Last night you were about to ask me something when Peggy came into the kitchen.'

'Was I?' he frowned. 'Oh, I remember. It was only to mention the talk. To tell you the truth, this is a new venture for me. I'm not used to speaking to this kind of audience and could do with your input.'

'You could? I'm afraid that what I know about ceramics, you could write on the back of a postage stamp, although I'm fascinated and would like to come.'

They had reached Aunt Rose who had managed to secure a table in the small designated area at the back of the church.

'Ah, well that's exactly it,' Keir continued, as he set down the cups of coffee. 'If Rose can spare you, I thought perhaps you could glance through my

notes tomorrow afternoon, see if they're on your wavelength. I'm quite passionate about my subject when I get going, but I don't want to get too technical.'

'So you want me to come along, so that you can practise on me — use me as a sounding board?'

Aunt Rose paused in her perusal of the church notice sheet.

'What a good idea. Well, you've certainly come to the right person. After all, Sophie is an English teacher, so she's got plenty of experience. If this young lady stays with me for too long she'll be fully occupied with all the demands on her time.'

Just then, Crystal and her mother came across and the conversation turned to other matters. Crystal gave Sophie a meaningful look as they were about to leave.

'Will I be seeing you in the library this week?'

'Yes, I ought to get myself some bedtime reading. I've just finished the paperback I brought with me,' Sophie replied, realising Crystal wanted to have a chat with her.

★ ★ ★

'Would you look at that!' exclaimed Aunt Rose, as they sat enjoying a television programme about antiques. 'That man's had that ugly old vase stashed away at the back of his cupboard and it's worth thousands! I wonder if Keir's watching this.'

'You haven't got a vase of Uncle Hugh's in the attic, have you?' Sophie teased.

'No, dear. I've thought about all the things he gave Tom and I over the years and the keepsakes that used to belong to Mary, but I can't come up with anything that has anything more than sentimental value.'

Sophie nodded sympathetically, having heard her parents say much the same thing.

'It's good that Keir's so keen to support local events, isn't it?' she remarked.

Aunt Rose nodded. 'We're lucky to have him around. He's an asset to the community. No wonder he and Hugh got along so well. He's a man after Hugh's own heart.'

Sophie stared at her. 'I'd no idea Keir knew Uncle Hugh. You haven't mentioned it before.'

'Haven't I, dear?' At times Aunt Rose could be infuriatingly vague, Sophie had discovered. 'Anyway, it's now that's important and I'm glad the two of you seem to be getting on so well.'

'So you won't mind if I go over to Rowanbank tomorrow afternoon, then?'

'Good gracious no. Anyway, Frances said she'd call in to discuss the Easter Fayre. It's a bit early, but she's a great believer in forward planning.'

# Staying On

As Sophie went through the hall on her way upstairs on Monday morning, she realised Aunt Rose was on the phone.

'It's your mother, Sophie. We've had a chat, so I'll pass you over — here she is, Anne. Bye for now.'

'Hi Mum, how are things your end?'

'Fine — what about you, dear? Rose sounds in good spirits.'

They chatted away for a minute or two and then Anne Burnett said, 'The main reason I'm ringing is because someone called Lynne, from the agency's, just phoned. She wasn't prepared to speak to me, so I fobbed her off by saying you were away for a few days and would get back to her ASAP. Apparently, she hasn't got your mobile number and I didn't like to give it to her without your permission.'

'Thanks, Mum. I've got the agency's

number here, so I'll get back to her now.'

'Look, love, if you want to take the job, I can come down to be with Rose for a few days.'

'Actually, Mum, I'm enjoying being here in Penbridge. There's quite a lot going on and I've met up with Crystal Briggs again. So if Aunt Rose doesn't mind, I think I might just stay on for a while longer.'

'Really? Well, I think you should consider paying Rose for your keep, if you do that, dear. She's a pensioner, after all.'

'Yes, I've already thought of that, but I'll need to be tactful. I've got a bit put away so I don't need to worry about finances just now. How much do you suggest?'

Anne chatted to her daughter for a bit longer ending by saying, 'I'm glad you're happy there, and Rose tells me she's enjoying your company. Anyway, if you change your mind let me know and I'll get straight in the car. It's fairly quiet here at the moment and Tim and your dad can fend for themselves for a while.'

'I'd be more than happy for you to stay as long as you feel able,' Aunt Rose told Sophie. 'It's lovely for me to have your company, but as for paying for your keep — I should be paying you for all the jobs you're doing for me.'

Sophie decided that when she went shopping she would pay for the purchases. It was the least she could do in the circumstances.

There was a sharp frost coating the grass like icing sugar. Aunt Rose decided to stay put and, after breakfast, Sophie assembled the ingredients for the Victoria sandwich Aunt Rose had insisted on making and, by the time the sun was making a watery appearance, the cake was cooling on its stand.

Sophie set off with a list and full instructions on how to get to the various places, including the farm shop.

'I usually get a lift with Mrs Cole from church, but she's got a bad cold,'

Aunt Rose had explained. 'Anyway, I've plenty to occupy me here until you get back. Take your time, dear. And I heard Crystal asking if you were going to call into the library. I've got another book to return, if you're going in that direction.'

Sophie realised she was going to have a busy morning and she hadn't even phoned the agency yet. She drove to the farm shop first and stocked up on fruit and vegetables, and then sat in the small car park and spoke to Lynne at the agency.

She was offered a post which started with immediate effect in a school, a few miles from the one she'd been working in. The member of staff had had an operation and was unlikely to be back at work this side of half term.

After she'd turned it down, Sophie sat for a few minutes longer, wondering if she'd made the right decision. She'd had no intention of staying more than a week or so when she'd first arrived in Penbridge, but there was something about the place that made her want to stay on. It was good meeting up with Crystal again. She smiled, and admitted to herself that, in spite of her better judgement, part of the attraction for staying on was Keir Ellison.

Having finished her shopping, Sophie popped into the library which was deserted, apart from a couple of students using the computers and an elderly lady selecting a large print book. Crystal grinned at Sophie.

'I was hoping you'd drop by. Do you fancy a coffee? We've just got time for a ten minute breather before the kiddies come for their story-telling session.'

Crystal called across to her assistant who was tidying one of the shelves and disappeared out the back to return, a few moments later, with two brightly coloured mugs and a packet of chocolate biscuits.

'Emma will have her break later. We take it in turns,' she explained. She lowered her voice. 'I think I've struck gold, Sophie. Alan's gorgeous. We went out again yesterday afternoon and it's all thanks to Keir.'

'I thought you two looked as if you were hitting it off on Saturday.'

'I'm not into blind dates as a rule, but Alan's so lovely, so how could I resist? Anyway, you seemed to be getting on well with Keir.'

'Oh, I should imagine Keir is one of those fellows who gets on well with everyone,' she said nonchalantly. 'He seems to have thrown himself into life round here.'

'So do I take it you'll be at his talk tomorrow night, then?'

'Yes, although I'm not sure about Aunt Rose. How about you?'

Crystal beamed. 'Alan's volunteered to do the visual aids so, yes, I certainly will.'

'Actually, I've been invited to Rowanbank this afternoon.' Sophie explained.

'You should be so honoured. Of course, I keep forgetting Hugh Mercer was a relative of yours.'

'Yes, he was my father's cousin, but

he was miles older, which is why my brother and I called him Uncle Hugh. Anyway, I doubt if that has any bearing on anything where Keir is concerned. He hadn't a clue who I was when I first turned up.'

'Well, he certainly does now — he got Mum to fill him in. She's a positive mine of information about local folk and their families.'

Sophie would have liked to question Crystal further — ask a few more questions about Keir — but she didn't want to give her the wrong impression. After all, it was just idle curiosity about the man who had come to live in her late uncle's house who seemed to be occupying more and more of her thoughts.

'It'll be interesting to find out what happens when Erica returns,' Crystal commented.

Startled, Sophie stared at her friend. 'How do you mean? Erica's not likely to return to Penbridge, is she? Now that she's sold Rowanbank.'

It was Crystal's turn to look surprised. 'But she hasn't sold Rowanbank. Whatever gave you that idea? She's just renting it out to Keir whilst she's in Spain. That's why it's still full of her things.'

Sophie tried to get her head round this.

'I'm sure Aunt Rose is under the impression that Keir's here for good.'

'Perhaps it's best left like that for the moment. After all, Mrs Harding didn't exactly hit it off with Erica, did she? Hugh Mercer had to go over to Rose Cottage if he wanted to see her.'

Sophie stared at Crystal, suddenly sensing there were things here that she didn't understand. Setting down her coffee mug, she returned Aunt Rose's book, selected a couple for herself, on Crystal's recommendation, and left just as several small children were being shepherded into the library by their parents.

Rowanbank was a red brick house built in the 1930s. Sophie hadn't set foot in it for a number of years, but she still felt a sense of pleasure as she stopped for a moment to admire it.

Keir ushered her into the study which was a small, book-lined room with a coal-effect gas fire, making it seem cosy. It had been Uncle Hugh's domain and, apart from the fire and some new plum-coloured, velvet curtains, Sophie didn't think it had changed much from when she'd previously seen it.

Keir sat opposite Sophie and shuffled some papers and, for the next hour, she listened and commented as he gave her an outline of his talk.

'I don't want to blind people with techniques or masses of history,' he explained. 'So I thought I'd just begin by giving a few examples of early pieces of pottery found in the area — show some illustrations of what they would have looked like originally — before moving on to stuff one might find in a church.'

Sophie frowned. 'You mean like a chalice or patten, but surely most of those were made from silver.'

'True, but some might have been ceramics. And then, there are the harvest jugs which are interesting. Moving on, I plan to touch briefly on the Staffordshire potteries and then show some slides to include Clarice Cliff and Moorcroft. I'll finish off by giving a few examples of my own efforts and those of my students. I also plan to have some work on display in one of the side rooms. What do you think?'

She nodded. 'It's fascinating, but you must have got enough material for several talks there.'

'Mmm, I'll obviously need to keep an eye on the clock. I'll round off the evening with a question and answer session, followed by refreshments for those who want to stay.'

'I'm looking forward to it,' Sophie assured him with a smile.

'Come into the sitting room and have some tea — thanks for your input, Sophie.'

Over tea, she surveyed the duck-egg

blue walls and the modern drapes and cream leather suite. Erica had certainly put her mark on things here. Sophie recalled the rather sober magnolia wallpaper and beige curtains that had been there previously and felt a sudden pang for how things used to be. The pictures were not to her taste either — gone were the gentle rural scenes, which had been replaced by rather bland Chinese prints.

Sophie wondered if they belonged to Keir, but somehow didn't think so.

As if reading her thoughts he said, 'Those are Erica's. Apart from a few of my personal possessions, everything's just as she left it.'

'Well, this room is certainly very different from the way I remember it. No wonder Aunt Rose gets a bit emotional when she mentions it.'

Keir gave her a steady look from rich brown eyes. 'But from what I understand, Rose would have opposed anything that Erica set out to do. They didn't exactly hit it off, did they?'

'That was hardly Aunt Rose's fault,' Sophie said, springing to the elderly lady's defence. 'I don't believe she was made to feel welcome at Rowanbank once Erica had got her feet under the table.'

'You don't appear to like Erica either,' he remarked. 'What's she done to you?'

'Nothing! I don't know what you mean. I scarcely know the woman. We only met on a couple of occasions. We weren't invited to the wedding, which apparently, was a very low key affair, but my family met up with Uncle Hugh and Erica for a meal when they were staying in St Albans. And then we met up with them again, when they were in London for one of Uncle Hugh's charity dos.'

Sophie was uncomfortably aware that Keir was studying her quizzically, a slight frown on his face.

'Anyway, what's it to you whether I like or dislike Erica? I suppose you're going to tell me you're a friend of hers.'

'Yes. Actually I am. She's allowing me to live at Rowanbank for a nominal rent whilst she's in Spain.'

Sophie stared at him open-mouthed. 'You mean Erica might be coming back here to live?' she asked, when she'd found her voice.

He shrugged. 'It's early days yet. She hasn't exactly found Penbridge a friendly place.'

'Then maybe she should either work at it a little harder or consider moving away for good and starting afresh,' Sophie said caustically, and then could have bitten her tongue, as she saw Keir's severe expression.

'Harsh words, Miss Burnett, but you don't know all the facts.'

Sophie stood up, eyes smouldering. 'I'm not sure I want to. But I do know none of my family have felt welcome here since Erica set foot in the place. It's as if she wanted to erase all that had gone before. Aunt Rose was deeply hurt by Erica's attitude and we're bound to support her.'

'Quite,' he said reasonably. 'I'm glad you're so loyal. This subject's obviously something we both beg to differ over, but that doesn't mean to say we can't be friends, does it?'

He caught her hands between his so that she was powerless to move, feeling the magnetism between them. Her eyes flashed as she surveyed him, long lashes sweeping her cheeks and he had a sudden overwhelming desire to kiss her, but instead found himself saying, 'Has anyone told you, you have the most beautiful eyes, and when you're angry they're magnificent.'

For a moment, he'd rendered her speechless. Her colour heightened and her heart beat painfully against her rib cage. She gave him a little smile.

'You can't win me over by turning on the charm, Keir Ellison,' she remarked, trying to keep her voice steady.

'No, but I can always try,' he rejoined and, bending forward, cupped her face in his hands and kissed her on the tip of her nose.

'Thanks for all your help with my talk, Sophie.'

'You're welcome,' she told him lightly, endeavouring to sound normal.

\* \* \*

'How did you get on, dear?' Aunt Rose enquired when Sophie entered the cottage shortly afterwards.

'Fine,' Sophie assured her. 'I can see what you mean about the way Erica's altered things.'

Aunt Rose sighed. 'Yes, well she's still young and obviously has very different tastes and ideas from Mary. Hugh kept things much the same over all those years, but things change. Probably Keir will put his stamp on things too.'

'You think he's planning to stay here then?'

'We'll have to wait and see, won't we? Time will tell. Anyway, I've had a productive afternoon. Frances has got some excellent ideas for the Easter Fayre.'

Sophie listened politely, but all the time, found her thoughts straying to Keir. He had been very much on the defensive where Erica was concerned, making it seem as if Aunt Rose was to blame for the rift in their relationship. Sophie didn't understand, and she was determined to get to the bottom of it.

As she got ready for bed that night, Sophie wondered if she'd been too hasty in turning down the job from the agency. After all, there might not be another suitable one for quite some time and, if things didn't work out here, she would regret her decision. Then she remembered the way Keir had looked at her, that slight moment of intimacy and knew that there was an undeniable chemistry between them. She sighed — if only Erica Mercer wouldn't keep coming between them. Sophie heartily wished Erica would remain in Spain for ever.

On an impulse, Sophie texted her brother, Tim, who was a notoriously late one for going to bed. He rang her within a couple of minutes.

'Hi, Soph how are things?'

She explained as briefly as possible.

'OK, well, I know even less than you about this Erica. I thought she'd sold Rowanbank.'

'So did I, but I suppose it would have been a bit quick. Anyway, apparently Keir Ellison's a friend of Erica's and seems to think our family have been a bit unfair towards her, but I can't see where he's coming from. Personally, I think there's a bit more to all of this than we're aware of.'

Tim whistled. 'Wasn't there something mysterious about those letters informing Mum and Dad and Aunt Rose that they'd already had something of value from Uncle Hugh, as if he was trying to tell them something from beyond the grave?'

'Don't be so melodramatic, Tim! If there was anything of value, don't you think Aunt Rose and our parents would have fathomed it out by now?'

'Perhaps that's what this guy, Keir

Whatsit, is doing — trying to suss it out for Erica.'

'Actually, I'm not really interested, Tim. Although it would have been nice if Aunt Rose could have had some recognition for all she'd done for Uncle Hugh over the years.'

'Are you talking to yourself in there, dear, or have you got a visitor?' came Aunt Rose's voice from the foot of the stairs.

'Sorry, Aunt Rose — just talking to Tim on my mobile — Tim, have a word with Aunt Rose.' She sped down the stairs and passed her mobile over.

Sophie lay awake for ages that night, going over the events of the day. Keir had seemed such a nice uncomplicated sort of person, but she should have realised from past experience that life was never that simple. Keir had insinuated that she was not in possession of all the facts about what had really caused the animosity between Erica and Aunt Rose. Sophie sighed — just as she was beginning to enjoy life here in Penbridge, this had cropped up. OK, she supposed she could do one of two things. Ignore the undercurrents and take each day as it came, or try to work out what they were all about.

★ ★ ★

The village hall was packed that evening. Fortunately, Crystal and Mavis Briggs had saved them a couple of seats fairly near the front.

'Good turn out, isn't it?' Crystal commented.

'So who are all these people?' asked Sophie, looking about her in surprise.

'Students from the various classes Keir works with, villagers and friends. He's popular.'

It was a fascinating talk and Sophie found herself watching Keir as he spoke and wondering again what had brought him to Penbridge. He looked incredibly handsome, his thick, fair hair contrasting with his dark jacket and blue striped, open-necked shirt. His voice was rich and clear, and she caught the enthusiasm for his subject in his tone.

When the talk had ended, the applause was deafening. After a question time, Keir announced that refreshments would be served adding, 'I've set up a small exhibition in the side room if you'd care to take a look. There's a variety of work from some of my present classes, together with one or two other items that I thought you might be interested in.'

Sophie managed to procure a couple of cups of coffee and was about to take them across to Aunt Rose when Keir skilfully added his own cup to the tray and removed it from her.

'Let me — so what did you think?'

'It all went very well,' she told him honestly. 'You've made me want to have a go myself.'

'So, why don't you?' His brown eyes met hers. 'Once the craft centre is up and running I intend to hold classes there but, until then, you'd be more than welcome to join my beginners' class. Crystal's going to come along.'

'I'd like that, but I'm not sure how long I'm going to be around,' she told him, acutely aware that she'd like to spend more time with him.

'OK, have a think about it and let me know,' he said as he distributed the coffee.

After a few minutes, Keir excused himself and went across to speak to another group of people. Aunt Rose was deep in conversation with Mavis Briggs, and Crystal and Alan were chatting to some members of Keir's evening class, so Sophie collected up the empty cups, returned them to the hatch and went to take a look at the ceramics exhibition which was being manned by several of Keir's students.

There was a wide selection of items, ranging from earrings and pendants to bowls and vases. Spotting some of Keir's work, Sophie bent to take a closer look. The bowls were exquisitely decorated in rich, jewel-like colours.

'Quite something, aren't they?' one of the students said. 'Keir's such a talented guy and we're learning so much from him.'

Sophie moved to the next display and was astonished to recognise some pieces from Rowanbank that had belonged to Hugh. She knew he'd enjoyed going to antique fairs and, in amongst some of the more modern items, realised there were likely to be some valuable antiques. She just hoped that no-one would damage them.

The crowd was thinning out when Keir caught up with her again.

'This exhibition is quite something,' she told him. 'Your students seem so enthusiastic. I really like your stuff, Keir — the colours are amazing.'

He touched her arm. 'Thanks, Sophie. I realise some people prefer pastel shades, but each to his own, eh?'

'Absolutely.' She hesitated. 'Keir, I'm sure it doesn't need me to tell you that some of these pieces that belonged to

Uncle Hugh's are — well, probably quite valuable.'

He looked startled. 'If that's your way of asking me to take care of them, then don't worry, I certainly will. But, what you probably don't realise is that Hugh left his collection to me so I can actually do exactly what I like with it — even sell it, if I so choose.'

Sophie felt herself colouring. She supposed this was Keir's way of telling her that it was no concern of hers. He gave Sophie an apologetic little smile as the red-head she'd seen talking to him outside the library beckoned to him.

Sophie's mind was working overtime. So Keir had been a close enough friend of Hugh's to be left his collection of ceramics. Unless of course, Erica had given it to Keir and he hadn't liked to mention that.

Sophie immediately dismissed that thought, realising it was highly improbable.

Turning back to the display, she found Aunt Rose and Mavis Briggs standing behind her and wondered if they'd heard her exchange with Keir. Fortunately, Aunt Rose gave no sign of having done so, but she studied the exhibits with a thoughtful expression on her face.

Just in case anyone was in any doubt, the label read that they were part of a collection that had belonged to the late Hugh Mercer.

'I thought Erica would have disposed of those long since,' Rose commented after a moment. 'It's good to know she hasn't.'

'You should try cleaning them,' Mavis Briggs said tartly. 'I'm always terrified of dropping the blessed things!'

'I'm surprised Erica's left them at Rowanbank. They must be worth a bob or two,' Rose remarked, echoing Sophie's thoughts. Sophie decided that now was not the right moment to divulge what Keir had just told her. She'd wait until she and Aunt Rose were back at Rose Cottage.

To Sophie's surprise, Tim rang up

again the following evening.

'Natalie's got a team-building course on Saturday, so I'm at a bit of a loose end. Mum said something about you needing more clothes so, if you like, I could come down to Penbridge to see you and Aunt Rose. What's going on, are you partying and if so who with?'

'Don't be daft,' she told him. 'I just need a few additional things in case of — of, well, who knows what might crop up. Anyway, it would be great to see you on Saturday.'

'Oh, and tell Aunt Rose not to worry about cooking a meal. Mum and Dad have offered to stand us lunch. Apparently, there's a rather good restaurant about a couple of miles out of Penbridge, but you might need to book.'

Aunt Rose was delighted. 'I haven't seen Tim for ages. Oh, what a nice surprise, but I'd willingly have made you lunch here. Can he stay over?'

'No, he's got to get back because he and his girlfriend have been invited out with friends on Sunday.'

On Thursday afternoon, Sophie went into the shop wondering what to expect. Peggy Munn spent the first twenty minutes showing her around the place and explaining her system, which seemed to be a kind of organised chaos.

Sophie was fascinated by the motley collection of things and browsed happily, all the time listening to Peggy Munn's chatter. The elderly lady seemed to be a font of information about village life.

'People pop in for a bit of a gossip sometimes, you know, and when school's over, parents bring their kiddies to spend their pocket money. I keep a selection of small items for them to choose from. Have you heard about that fancy place they're talking of opening in Bridge Street?'

'Well, yes, it's actually going ahead, isn't it?'

Peggy Munn sniffed. 'All these people with their new-fangled ideas. What we need is a place for the farmers' market. Well, they needn't think they'll drive me out of business!'

'Would you like me to do a bit of dusting or tidying?' Sophie asked hurriedly, deciding it might be best to change the subject.

'You can if you like, dear, but you will be careful, won't you?'

Sophie was in the middle of reorganising one of the displays of glassware when the door opened and Keir came into the shop.

His eyebrows rose when he saw her. 'Well, you don't look like Mrs Munn.'

'She's out the back making some tea — did you want me to fetch her?'

'No hurry — just wondering if I'd had any sales. Mind if I take a look?'

He went across to the show case. 'Goodness! There's a surprise — four items sold in a week!'

'I expect it was your talk that did it. Everyone will want to own a piece of Keir Ellison pottery now.'

He chuckled. 'I wish! Look about that — I think I owe you a bit of an explanation.'

He came to stand beside her. 'Those pieces Hugh left me — well, they meant a lot to him, and he knew I'd treasure them. I want you to know that they're in safe hands and I've got absolutely no intention of selling them.'

'None of my business,' she said quickly, very aware of his closeness, of his sheer maleness. She caught a waft of his cologne — fresh and woody.

'Let me assure you that they mean a lot to me too, particularly the modern collection.' A shadow crossed his face. 'Hugh and I both knew the potter. She was a very talented and lovely young woman who died just as she was beginning to gain recognition.'

He sighed. 'Erica isn't much into ceramics — her tastes are vastly different, as you can tell from the paintings and prints, which is another reason why Hugh left his collection to me. Anyway, I just wanted you to know.'

He put out a hand and touched Sophie's arm, the contact making her want to cry out.

Was he aware of the effect he had on her? She pulled herself together with an effort, just as Peggy Munn came into the room bearing a tea tray.

'Hello Mr — er, Keir — would you like a cup of tea?'

He declined graciously, collected his payment and left a moment or two later.

'Such a nice young man. Talented too,' Peggy Munn remarked for the second time, as she passed the custard creams. 'I suppose I couldn't blame him if he wanted to take his business to this new place, although if everyone did that, then I know it'd be curtains for me.'

Her rheumy eyes misted and Sophie wished she could think of something to console the elderly lady, but failed, realising that, in all probability, it would prove to be an inevitable outcome.

# 'I Happen to Like it Here'

Tim turned up at eleven-thirty on Saturday, just in time to unload the car and have a quick chat with Aunt Rose before whisking them off to the restaurant where Sophie had booked a table. It was situated in a beautiful spot just south of Penbridge. They could see for miles across a patchwork of ploughed fields. The landscape was still rather bleak, but in a month or so, it would spring into life.

They were halfway through their main course when the door opened and a group of people came in, amongst them Alan and Crystal, who paused by their table.

'Tim, how lovely to see you! It must be years!' Crystal exclaimed and introduced Alan.

'Keir's evening class are having a belated Christmas meal. Alan's asked

109

me along because I'm joining the class as someone's dropped out.'

A few minutes later, the door opened again and Keir appeared accompanied by the red-haired Glenda who was wearing a white, fur-trimmed jacket, a short skirt and long fashion boots. Keir stopped to speak, but before he could do any more than briefly acknowledge them Glenda said rudely, 'Come on, Keir; everyone's waiting for you.'

And with a brief, apologetic smile, he was gone.

Tim pursed his lips in a silent whistle. 'Who on earth was that?'

'Aunt Rose's next door neighbour, Keir Ellison, who's renting Rowanbank whilst Erica's away.'

'Yes, I gathered that. I actually meant the red-head? Is she his girlfriend?'

'Oh, she's just one of his students,' supplied Aunt Rose, 'although in my day, students treated their tutors with a bit more respect.'

'Well, she actually attends his beginners' evening class and I think that's quite informal,' Sophie pointed out, wondering if there really was anything going on between them. Glenda was certainly very attractive and was doing her best to flirt with Keir. As Sophie heard the gales of laughter coming from the table occupied by Keir's class, she felt a little prickle of jealousy.

It was an excellent meal and afterwards, they went back to Rose Cottage. When Aunt Rose got up to feed Poppy, Tim said, 'I'll just take your case upstairs, Sophie, so that I can return it to Mum.'

'What was all that about?' Sophie demanded, a few minutes later as they sat in her room. 'Mum said I could keep the case for the time being.'

'I couldn't think of any other excuse to get to talk to you on your own. What's going on, Soph? You're a townie not someone to bury herself in a backwater like Penbridge for any length of time. It's not like you to turn down the chance of some work either.'

'Perhaps I want a bit of time to chill out,' Sophie told him rather sharply. 'Anyway, I happen to like it here. There's a lot going on and it makes a change from being in the rat race. Just don't read too much into it.'

'But you've asked me to bring your laptop and Mum to pack your business suit — are you going for an interview or something?'

Sophie shrugged. 'Who knows what I might do. It's good to have the right clothes — and be prepared, just in case something crops up. I can't go on living with Mum and Dad for ever and I need a bit of time out to think things through.'

'If you say so. You can't stay here for ever either. Once Aunt Rose is fully mobile again you won't have any reason to stay.'

'Aunt Rose says she's enjoying my company,' Sophie informed him. 'You'd better take my smaller case back with you.'

Tim was looking at her curiously, 'Is

there something you're not telling me, Soph?'

'Of course not,' she assured him, 'at least . . . ' She filled him in about Keir and the ceramics. 'I am a bit surprised that Uncle Hugh left his collection of ceramics to Keir and didn't leave us a bean. It makes me sound mercenary and it isn't intended, but . . . '

'Aunt Rose wasn't left anything either, was she?'

'No, she only received the same sort of letter as Mum and Dad. The solicitor couldn't make any sense of it either. You should see the inside of Rowan-bank, Tim, you wouldn't recognise the place.'

'Tea!' Aunt Rose shouted up the stairs, a few moments later, and Sophie stuffed a couple of unwanted garments and some books she'd finished with into the case and they went downstairs again.

★　★　★

113

As Tim was leaving he said in Sophie's ear, 'If it all gets too much for you, or you want me to suss anything out, give me a buzz.'

Sophie smiled at him. It was good to have such a caring brother. She knew she could depend on him. She didn't know what the future held for her, but somehow felt Penbridge was the right place to be just now, although seeing Keir Ellison with Glenda at lunch-time had made her feel strangely unsettled again.

'Of course you can stay for as long as you like,' Aunt Rose reiterated when Sophie broached the subject that evening. 'I love having you here — you've been such a help. I'm just worried that you'll find it dull. It's hardly the right time of year to go out anywhere.'

'Well, as soon as the weather bucks up we can go for a spin in the car,' Sophie told her, picking up the tea tray.

At church the following morning, Mrs Briggs came across to Rose.

'I've got a very big favour to ask you, Rose. The teachers at my little grand-daughter's school have got one of those staff development days, or whatever they call them nowadays, tomorrow, and I'm at Rowanbank in the morning — so I was wondering . . . '

'Oh, bring her over to Rose Cottage, Mavis. We'd be delighted to keep an eye on her, wouldn't we, Sophie?'

Sophie smilingly agreed before turning back to Crystal, with whom she'd been having a chat. 'So are you going out with Alan today?'

'No, he's gone with Keir and a group of students to an art exhibition. They did ask me, but I've only known Alan a week and don't want him to think I'm being too full on. Besides, Teresa and Steve are coming to lunch with little Amy.'

'I expect Glenda's going to the exhibition,' Sophie said, before she could prevent herself.

'You bet she is! She's a dreadful flirt and, although Keir's always friendly, he certainly doesn't encourage her. He's a perfect gentleman — pleasant to everyone. It's my belief he's got someone tucked away in the background.'

After lunch Aunt Rose said she wanted to watch something on TV, so Sophie decided to go out for a walk.

Fiona and Ian Knight were in their front garden. She'd met them at Keir's talk.

'Hi, we've just been for a walk too. Are you staying here for a while?'

'Just until Aunt Rose is fully mobile.'

'Yes, we're sorry we didn't realise she'd had an accident,' Fiona said sympathetically.

'We're pleased we managed to get to Keir's talk the other day,' Ian told Sophie. 'We can't wait for the craft centre to get up and running. It'll be a boost for the village.'

'Do you think so? I'm worried it'll take business away from Peggy Munn.'

They chatted for a few more minutes then Sophie headed back to the cottage.

The following morning Sophie had

just set off to collect Amy from Rowanbank when she bumped into Keir accompanied by a small figure.

'We suddenly realised Amy had never met you, so I've brought her across.'

'Where's that other lady?' asked Amy. 'The one with the yellow hair?'

'Oh, you mean Erica, Mrs Mercer?'

'Mrs Mercer's gone to Spain with her friend.'

They all made their way to Rose Cottage.

★ ★ ★

Aunt Rose looked up with a smile. 'Hello Amy, just the person I could do with. Do you think you could help me make some peg dolls?'

The little girl nodded and perched herself on a stool beside Aunt Rose. A few minutes later the grey and blonde heads were bent over their work.

'Well, it looks as if we're redundant,' said Keir.

Aunt Rose's head shot up. 'Oh, no

you're not. You can fetch me that large cardboard box from the cupboard under the stairs.'

'Did you enjoy the exhibition yesterday?' Sophie asked as he extracted the box.

'To be perfectly honest I found it a bit disappointing, but most of the others liked it so that was good and, after all, it's important for my students to get to see a wide variety of different aspects of ceramics.' He glanced at his watch. 'Unfortunately, I'm going to have to go very shortly or I'll never get the work ready for this wretched meeting this afternoon.'

Keir placed the box within easy reach of Rose, and Sophie felt a pang of disappointment as he made a quick exit before Amy noticed. Luckily the child was so absorbed in what she was doing that she didn't even look up.

Midway through the morning, Sophie glanced at Aunt Rose and saw how tired she was looking. Summing up the situation Sophie said, 'Shall I put the kettle on? I'm sure this young lady would like a hot blackcurrant drink and I expect you're ready for your coffee?'

'What a good idea,' Aunt Rose said, looking relieved, 'and there are some chocolate biscuits in the tin.'

After their elevenses, Sophie volunteered to read Amy a story and then the little girl produced her own reading book and they had some quiet time whilst Aunt Rose carried on working on her dolls' house furniture.

Later on, Sophie took Amy into the garden to let off steam. Aunt Rose had found an old tennis ball and a couple of racquets in the cupboard.

Amy was an energetic child and obviously good at sport. They spent a hectic half hour careering round the garden and then, much to Sophie's embarrassment, she saw Keir watching them from the back door.

He thought what a picture Sophie looked. Her hair was all over the place and her cheeks were rosy. He smiled to himself, thinking how refreshingly natural and unsophisticated she was and knowing he was attracted to her.

Nina had been the love of his life and he'd vowed there would never be anyone else, but that was before he'd met Sophie Burnett. Keir snapped out of his reverie and called to Amy. The little girl ran up to him.

'Your grandmother's almost ready to leave now, Amy, and I've got to go to my meeting soon.'

Amy pulled a face. 'Oh — can I come with you?'

'I'm afraid not, it'll be very boring and you wouldn't like it at all. No, you'd be much happier staying with your grandmother.'

'I've had a brill time this morning. Can I come again, Sophie?'

'I'm sure you can, but you'll have to ask Mrs Harding because it's her cottage, you see.'

'You're very welcome, lovey,' Aunt Rose said, a few minutes later, when Amy skipped indoors and repeated her question. 'Now, are you going to take these peg dollies with you?'

It was Sophie's turn to stand and watch from the back door, as the child set off with Keir. When they reached the gate they turned and waved.

'There goes one very nice young man,' Aunt Rose commented, echoing Sophie's thoughts. The problem was — he seemed too nice. There was another tick in the tick box — he was good with children too. Sophie knew she was becoming increasingly attracted to him and she was powerless to do anything about it.

The week fell into some kind of routine after that. Aunt Rose felt able to accompany Sophie to the farm shop, but declined Sophie's suggestion that she might like to go further afield perhaps into Tonbridge.

'When the weather improves, and I feel more confident walking on this foot, then there'll be no stopping me but, for the moment, I'm happy to stay in Penbridge. But don't let me stop you from having a wander round. There are quite a few things I could do with, if you do get near one of the supermarkets.'

Sophie realised that she was soon going to have to make a decision about what she intended to do. She loved being in Penbridge, but couldn't impose on Aunt Rose for ever.

That afternoon she popped into the village to get a few essential groceries for Aunt Rose and decided to call in to the library.

Crystal beamed at her. 'Thanks for looking after Amy on Monday. She had a wonderful time. Don't tell me Mrs Harding's finished all her library books already!'

'No, I just called in for a few minutes' natter.'

Crystal leaned across the counter. 'OK, we're not exactly rushed off our feet, as you can see, although we were quite busy this morning, and we had a group of school children in, up until half-an-hour ago, from the local primary school.'

'Crystal, I've decided to stay in Penbridge for a while, but I'll obviously need to get some work. Have you got any ideas?'

Crystal thought for a moment. 'There's always plenty of voluntary work, but paid — that's a very different matter. You might pick up a few waitressing shifts at that restaurant we all went to the other Saturday or there's a garden centre. You could ask there. I'm so pleased you're wanting to stay, Sophie. I'm going to my first evening class with Keir tonight. I'm sure you'd be welcome to come along too.'

'Oh, I'm not sure if . . . ' Sophie began.

Just then an elderly couple came up to the desk with an enquiry and Sophie said goodbye to Crystal and left. The idea of spending more time with Keir was tantalising, but the thought of watching Glenda flirting with him made Sophie feel reluctant to join the class.

On Thursday afternoon, Sophie did another stint at the gift shop and this time, she managed to persuade Peggy Munn to allow her to do something about the window display which was faded and rather unappealing.

Under her direction, Sophie removed all the items and carefully placed them in the small kitchen and then, leaving Peggy to wash them, Sophie cleaned the inside of the window and removed quantities of dusty lining paper. She spent a pleasant time creating the background for a new display.

Looking up, she saw Keir grinning at her from the street. She clambered out of the window as he entered the shop. Her heartbeat quickened at the sight of him. She dusted her hands on her jeans, aware that she must look spectacularly untidy.

'Well, you look busy and, er, rather dusty,' he said.

She coloured. 'So would you be, but at least you can see in the window.'

'I'm full of admiration for your diligence,' he teased.

'Have you brought us some more of

your ceramics?' she asked, eyeing the bulging bags he was carrying.

'I certainly have, together with just a few pieces from my students this time. They're so keen to display their work. Do you suppose Mrs Munn could be persuaded to let us put them in the window?'

'I can ask her, but don't hold your breath. She was planning to put back all the things we've removed, probably in the same order.'

He laughed, and reaching up, rubbed her cheek gently. 'You've got a speck of dirt just there. That's better.'

She caught her breath at his touch. She knew she felt an undeniable attraction towards him. Perhaps she was truly over Brett or was it just that Keir was such a charmer?

He cast his eyes about the shop now and she wondered what he was looking for. 'That indigo chenille cloth would make a perfect foil for our display.'

She followed his gaze and her eyes widened. 'You are joking — that table's full of china! How am I expected to shift it, even if Mrs Munn agreed? Anyway, I've just spent ages recovering the shelving in the window. You really are the giddy limit, Keir.'

'I know,' he said with a devastating smile which made her go weak at the knees. He flung an arm about her shoulder. 'Humour me, I've just had a brilliant idea.'

Sophie pulled a face at him. 'You have? OK, but if it means undoing what I've just spent the last couple of hours doing then I don't want to know.'

'Where's Mrs Munn?' he asked, taking no notice of this last comment.

'Out the back. She was supposed to be washing the ornaments, but last time I looked she was having a snooze. Why?'

'Then there's no time to lose.' Keir removed his jacket and carefully began to dismantle the display of china ornaments.

For a moment Sophie just gaped at him and then she said, 'Keir you can't just barge in here and change things round without even asking.'

He patted her shoulder. 'Trust me. I know what I'm doing.'

His closeness sent her pulse racing. 'OK, but on your own head be it. This has nothing to do with me!'

'Come on. I could do with another pair of hands.'

She hesitated for a moment and then took the ornaments he handed her and placed them carefully on the floor.

'Time is of the essence,' he said. 'Can you take this cloth into the garden and shake it?'

'Hardly, I'd wake Mrs Munn.'

His eyes glinted. 'Then you'll just have to go out the front. Don't argue, Sophie. We haven't got all day.'

Sophie opened her mouth to retort and found herself meekly obeying. She was beginning to discover that Keir had a way of getting people to do his bidding. She wasn't sure whether to be angry or amused at his nerve.

Fortunately there was hardly anybody about as she stood shaking the heavy cloth free of dust. She returned to the shop and gave Keir a hand to get it on the shelf in the window.

They had just finished arranging the pieces of pottery when Peggy Munn came into the shop. 'Oh, dear. I must have fallen asleep. Hello Keir, whatever are you up to?'

He turned on the charm and, taking her by the arm, steered her gently outside of the shop, leaving Sophie to follow.

'Well!' Peggy Munn exclaimed, gazing at the window display. 'I have to say you've made a very good job of it, but you're very naughty taking advantage of me falling asleep like that.'

Keir looked contrite. 'I'll dismantle it all, if that's what you want.'

She chuckled. 'You know how to twist me round your little finger, don't you? But just tell me whatever I'm supposed to do with all that stuff you've left on my shop floor?'

'How long have you had it?' he asked as they went back inside.

Peggy Munn sighed. 'Too long. I can't seem to shift it.'

'Well, I might be able to help you there. One of my evening class students has a bric-a-brac stall in one of the markets. If we box this lot up, I'll see if we can sell it for you — that's if you're in agreement, and then the stuff that was in the window can go back on display here.'

'No, I've made my mind up that can go as well — thank you, Keir. I'd have a bit more space without that table in here, wouldn't I?'

As Sophie and Keir left the shop a little later, Keir paused to look at the window display again. 'Well, that's looking pretty good, don't you think?'

Sophie nodded. 'Just so long as you're not planning to remove your pottery from the shop once the craft centre is up and running, and leave Peggy Munn high and dry. It's as well she isn't going for a makeover or she could be well and truly out of pocket.'

Keir saw the reproach in her

beautiful eyes and had an overwhelming desire to take her in his arms and kiss that lovely mouth and quell her fears. Instead he said, 'That's a bit harsh, isn't it? I'm sorry if you think that, Sophie. Not everyone has an ulterior motive, you know,' and he shot off towards the car park, leaving her staring after him and wishing she could have retracted the comments.

\* \* \*

Sophie had a long chat with her mother on the phone that evening.

'Darling, I've got a bit of a problem on my hands,' Anne Burnett told her daughter.

'What's wrong, Mum?'

'Are you still happy to stay with Rose for the time being?'

'Well, yes, although if I stay too much longer I'll need to get some work. Why, have you let my room out?'

'Not exactly, but you're on the right lines. Your Uncle Tom's going to

America on business for a few weeks and Aunt Judy's got the opportunity of going with him. The thing is, Sophie, they don't like to leave your gran on her own, so I've said she can come to us.' Anne Burnett paused. 'For about a month.'

'Gran — a month! Then I'd better come home. You'll need some help.'

'No, I'll manage perfectly and it will be good to have some quality time with my mother. The thing is, Sophie, it'll be easier to put her in your room than Tim's. His is always in a perpetual muddle and I don't think she'd like the colour scheme!'

Sophie was silent for several seconds and her mother said, 'Sophie are you still there?'

'Yes, I'm just trying to get my head round this. So, even if I wanted to come home, there wouldn't be any space?'

'Of course there would, dear, there's always the put-you-up downstairs or Tim could sleep there and you could have his room.'

'No way! I'd like to see Gran though — it's been ages.'

'Well, you could always come up for a weekend. Anyway think about it. But, I do need to know about your room by the weekend.'

'Tim could always go to stay with Natalie,' Sophie suggested.

'Yes, he has suggested that,' Anne Burnett said doubtfully, 'but Natalie's parents have got both her brothers also living in that small terraced house already.'

When Sophie came off the phone she went to speak to Aunt Rose.

'Sophie, you know I love you being here. If I could afford to pay you to be my companion, I would. You're a wonderful help and I enjoy your company, but you need to get out and about.'

At Sophie's insistence, they discussed a reasonable amount of money for her to pay into the house-keeping purse each week and, having burnt her boats for the next month, Sophie decided to set about finding herself some form of work.

After an early lunch on Saturday, Sophie set off for the village to pick up Aunt Rose's bread order and to settle the paper bill. It was chilly, but a watery sun filtered through the clouds. Sophie took a deep breath. It was a good mile into the village, but she was glad of some exercise. She was halfway along the lane when Keir's red Vauxhall pulled up in front of her.

'Going anywhere in particular?' he enquired.

'Just the village — one or two errands to run for Aunt Rose.'

'Are you in a hurry?'

'No, why are you intending to delay me?'

Keir laughed. 'Hop in, there's somewhere special I'd like to show you. It won't take long.'

Intrigued, Sophie climbed into the car and settled herself beside him.

'This sounds very curious. You haven't changed Peggy's window back again, have you?'

'What?' He chuckled. 'No. Have you forgiven me, yet?'

'I'm not sure. You are rather high-handed you know,' she teased.

'Goodness, no-one's ever told me that before. I'll have to think about that one. Now, I wonder where I can park.'

'Where are you taking me?' Sophie asked. Keir had waited patiently whilst she'd collected the bread, paid for the newspapers and stowed them away in the car. And then he had marched her off down a side street. He didn't answer and she had to hurry to keep pace with him. A few minutes later, he stopped in front of an elderly looking building.

Several cars were pulled up outside. Keir raised his hand in greeting to someone standing by the door.

'This,' he told Sophie proudly, 'is the old chapel, soon to be the new craft centre. I thought if you took a look inside you might get a clearer idea of what we're proposing.'

Sophie stood stock still. 'You're

hoping to get me on your side, you mean! What I don't understand is why you would take all this trouble to fight for this cause, when you're not a local, and are only living here on a temporary basis.'

He looked at her in astonishment. 'I can't believe you just said that, Sophie Burnett! You're not a local either and you're also living here temporarily. What's the difference? Am I missing something?'

'Yes, I've known Aunt Rose and Peggy Munn all my life. When we were children, my brother and I used to come to Penbridge with our parents, to stay with Uncle Hugh and Aunt Mary, so this village and the people in it are special to me and I don't like to see things spoilt.'

'Nor do I,' he said gently. 'The problem is, time marches on whether we like it or not and sometimes change is for the best. I really do have other people's interests at heart, you know, but there are one or two things I can't talk about quite yet, not until I'm quite certain they'll come to fruition.' He slung an arm about her shoulder. 'Trust me, Sophie, that's all I'm asking you to do.'

She caught her breath, feeling as if his fingers were burning into her flesh. The magnetism between them was palpable. Was she being disloyal to Aunt Rose for allowing him to try to influence her like this?

'OK, but you're going to have your work cut out to convince me,' she said shakily. 'Come on then show me inside this building.'

She followed him inside where a group of people were assembled. They greeted Keir and some of them looked curiously at Sophie.

'This is Sophie Burnett. She's staying with my neighbour and I've invited her to take a look round, because Hugh Mercer was her father's cousin and we all know how passionate he was about this place becoming a craft centre.'

There was a murmur of agreement.

Sophie was surprised. It was the first she'd heard of Uncle Hugh's interest in the place.

'As you can see, Sophie, they've made a good start on the alterations and we hope to have the whole thing up and running by Easter.'

'So soon.' Sophie was amazed. She supposed she must have been inside the old chapel before, but couldn't remember. The leader of the group pointed out the various areas that had been marked out and they all pored over a plan pinned to the wall.

Reluctantly, Sophie had to admit to herself that she could certainly see the possibilities, plenty of room, lots of light, well situated.

'So what do you think?' Keir asked her, as they wandered round the space with its high roof.

'It's a bit difficult to envisage what it might look like when it's finished, but yes, I'm sure it's got a lot of potential,' she conceded reluctantly. 'And obviously, you've got enough people interested to make it a viable proposition. They're all very keen, aren't they?'

Keir nodded. 'They certainly are. There are several artists and craftsmen living in this vicinity. But it's so much more than that, Sophie . . . '

He trailed off as a tall, thin man with greying hair approached them.

'Hello, John — good to see you here. Sophie this is John Munn — Peggy Munn's son. If anyone was opposed to this idea at the outset, he was.'

'So what made you change your mind?' Sophie asked curiously.

John stroked his chin. 'Oh, I could see I was fighting a lost cause. I mean, there's so much enthusiasm from this lot. Anyway, I thought, if you can't beat 'em join 'em. Deep down, I realised my old mother would have to face facts sooner or later. That shop is getting beyond her nowadays, but she's loved being there and it's given her a purpose in life since my father died. We've been talking to her about moving into a bungalow in a sheltered accommodation complex near us for some while now, but it has to be her decision.'

'It's unfortunate things can't stay as they are for ever,' Keir put in, 'but that little shop is in a bit of a timewarp, John.'

He nodded. 'I guess so. I'm afraid it just isn't paying its way. I'm grateful for what you've done, by the way — the pair of you. That window's looking fantastic and I don't know how you've managed to get Mum to part with some of that clutter, Keir. She's an unbelievable hoarder and you've achieved more than my wife and I have managed in months. My mother can be rather stubborn about change.'

'We enjoyed ourselves, didn't we, Sophie?'

'We certainly did. We were only too pleased to help,' she affirmed.

'I think my mother saw herself as being in the shop until the end of her days, but we've gently pointed out this might be a golden opportunity for her to have a bit of time out. She's always wanted to visit her cousins in Devonshire and used the shop as an excuse for not going. We'd be only too happy to take her there.'

'So, you really believe that once this venture is up and running it would be the end for the gift shop?' Sophie persisted.

John rubbed his ear. 'Not immediately, but this place would be a much better outlet for people's work — more spacious — you must surely see that. We feel it would be better for Mum to move now, rather than wait until business grinds to a halt altogether.'

'And what about Aunt Rose's dolls' house furniture? Where would she sell that?' demanded Sophie.

The two men exchanged meaningful looks and she wondered why.

'Look, let's not worry about any of that just now,' Keir told her. 'As John has said, the craft centre's not going to be completed overnight. I'm sure we'll come up with some solution by the time it's up and running.'

# A Stolen Kiss

As they made to leave the centre, Keir took Sophie's arm and gave her a keen look from his expressive brown eyes, sending her heart thumping against her ribcage.

'Thanks for coming with me, Sophie. I know it's a lot to take on board in one go, but I think it's a very worthwhile project.'

'Actually, I didn't have much option, did I?' she said unsteadily. 'You virtually frog-marched me here and didn't say where we were going.'

She saw his expression and added, 'Oh, don't worry, it's been an enlightening experience. I always like to understand both sides of an argument, but don't think you can win me round that easily!'

'I wouldn't dream of it,' he told her evenly, meeting her grey eyes steadily with his, so that her pulse raced. 'You're much too intelligent a person to allow yourself to be brainwashed.'

'And as I've told you before, you're not going to win me over by flattery either,' she told him firmly. 'I form my own opinions in my own good time. Anyway, I've found it both interesting and thought-provoking.'

'Well that's something I suppose,' he said, squeezing her arm, and she caught a glint in his eyes. 'All this talking and the dusty atmosphere has made me thirsty. I really fancy sitting by a log fire with toast and jam.'

'In your dreams — that sounds like nursery tea straight out of Enid Blyton.'

He laughed. 'Mmn, and I know just the place — is Rose waiting for that bread?'

'No, she's going to be deeply entrenched in making her dolls' house furniture this afternoon, and she loses all track of time when she gets involved — why?'

'Do you fancy having tea with me

back at Rowanbank?'

'You haven't got a log fire, have you?'

'Only an artificial one, but it's very realistic and I can offer toasted muffins and some of Mrs Briggs' cherry jam. Seriously, Sophie, I think it's about time I filled you in on one or two more things of which you're obviously not aware.'

Sophie shot him a surprised look, realising that, in spite of her reservations, she really wanted to get to know more about this man and wondered what he was going to tell her.

She gave Aunt Rose a quick ring on her mobile, and then they set off for Rowanbank.

As they sat over tea in the cosy little study, Keir said, 'As I've already told you there are one or two things you ought to know. Unfortunately, I can't explain everything quite yet, because I'm not the only one involved but . . . '

'Involved in what?' she demanded, wondering what on earth he was talking about.

He hesitated and Sophie thought he looked uncomfortable.

'Sophie, I realise you're aware there was no love lost between Erica and Rose. Have you any idea why that was?'

She stared at him in surprise. 'No, and it's none of my business. If Aunt Rose wants to tell me then, no doubt, she will. Anyway, it's all water under the bridge now that Uncle Hugh has died. I suspect it was partly because Erica and Aunt Rose are very different people. Aunt Rose was very fond of Uncle Hugh. After all, she'd known him from childhood so they were great friends and she would have wanted to protect his interests. She spent a lot of time in his company before he remarried and, to be honest, I think she saw Erica as — as . . . '

'As a gold-digger?' he suggested, and Sophie coloured, because he had come up with exactly the phrase she'd been trying to avoid.

'Well, sort of, I suppose. I don't remember much about Aunt Mary, but

I know that she was more like Aunt Rose — which is understandable, as they were twins and had that special bond. Anyway, what are you driving at?'

'I think Rose thought that Erica influenced Hugh's thinking — tried to manipulate him into doing what she wanted.'

'Well, didn't she?' Sophie demanded.

Keir shook his head. 'Hugh was very much his own man. Oh, he let Erica have her head when it came to redecorating Rowanbank, but let's be fair. She wouldn't have wanted to be reminded of Hugh's first wife, Mary, everytime she stepped into a room, would she now?

'I'm afraid the thing your Aunt Rose found hard to digest was that Hugh and Erica really cared about each other and had a lot in common on many issues. They actually had a good marriage, even though it was painfully short. But, leaving that aside, Hugh was passionate about the craft centre. It was his vision — I'm afraid Rose and he fell out over it, which is why the situation needs handling with kid gloves where she's concerned.'

Sophie stared at Keir, as his words registered. 'I've never heard any mention of Uncle Hugh and Aunt Rose falling out. It was Erica who dissuaded her from going across to Rowanbank by making her feel so unwelcome.'

His eyes narrowed. 'Yes, well, let's not go into all that. I suspect there were faults on both sides, but believe you me, I'm right in what I'm telling you over the craft centre. Hugh was heavily involved in making it viable — sitting on a committee, applying for a grant, that sort of thing. He was a very influential character.'

Sophie cupped her hands round the mug of tea. 'Yes, I'm aware of that, but why would Aunt Rose object so strongly that they fell out over it?'

'She was clinging onto the past, I suppose. She and her husband had built up the dolls' house furniture business from scratch. Oh, there's been opposition from several other people who've also used Peggy Munn's shop as an outlet for their own wares. Like Rose, they suspect that Peggy Munn's business will dwindle once the craft centre is up and running. They argue that they couldn't afford to display their goods anywhere else, if that happens.'

Sophie sighed. 'And they're probably right, aren't they? So can you blame them for being prejudiced? It's such a pity both businesses can't run in harmony with one another, but I'm aware, from what John Munn says, that Peggy might be considering retiring soon anyway. And what about Erica? I can't believe she hasn't had any input in all of this!'

Keir leant forward in his chair. 'Naturally. She's always supported Hugh's projects and she's very pro the craft centre because it was his dream, although she'll openly admit that she isn't overly interested in ceramics, which is why Hugh left me his collection and not her. Since Hugh died she's taken a back seat and left it to others to carry out his vision.'

'Namely you?' she asked, as light suddenly dawned. 'That's why you've come here, isn't it — to see that Uncle Hugh's wishes are carried out.'

For a moment he didn't reply and, watching him, Sophie thought a shadow crossed his face.

'Partly,' he told her at length, 'but I needed a change of environment, the same as you, and so I thought that Penbridge was the ideal place for me to be for the time being.'

Sophie swallowed. 'What makes you think I needed a change of environment?' she asked, trying to keep her voice steady.

His eyes met hers. 'It doesn't take much to fathom that one out. You're a teacher — this is term time. I suspect you're escaping from something — a relationship that didn't work out perhaps? Am I right?'

Sophie found his probing gaze disconcerting. The colour flooded her cheeks and turning away she said quietly, 'It's none of your business. Aunt Rose needed a pair of hands. I was available to help and I happen to like Penbridge. How about you?'

'Me? I like Penbridge too.'

Sophie noticed Keir was slightly uncomfortable when the questions were directed at him. She still wasn't ready to talk about Brett. It was so much easier to stay on neutral ground, and she suspected he felt the same way about whatever it was that haunted him.

They lapsed into silence.

'Thanks for the tea,' she said a few minutes later. 'Now I really had better get back to Rose Cottage before it gets too dark.'

Keir got to his feet and peered out of the window. 'It already has — I'll walk you back. I've got a flashlight.'

'There's no need. It's not that far,' she told him, not wanting to appear too eager.

'Sophie, I insist. You never know what

might be lurking out there — leopards, wolves, dragons.'

Sophie burst out laughing. 'Don't be ridiculous! OK, you win. Don't forget your sword!'

'No need, you can just whack them with the bread!'

He leant towards her and for one mad, heart-stopping moment she thought he was going to kiss her, but instead he caught her hands between his.

'Sophie, I really hope what I've said hasn't made any difference to us being friends.'

'Why would it?' she asked, her heart beating a wild tattoo.

'That's good, because I like your company. Actually, I was hoping you might come to the village dance with me on Saturday.'

'Great,' she said, trying to sound casual. 'I'll look forward to that.'

He walked her back to Rose Cottage, tucking his arm through hers, and her heart sang. It didn't matter what had happened in the past between Erica and

Rose or even Uncle Hugh. That had nothing to do with her. This promised to be a new beginning and she wasn't going to let anyone or anything spoil it.

* ★ ★ ★ *

'Keir's asked you to the dance? Brilliant — I'm going with Alan. There's usually quite a crowd. It's a popular event because there's not much else going on this time of the year.'

It was Crystal's afternoon off and they were sitting over lunch in her mother's kitchen.

'So what do I wear? Is it dressy or will my long black skirt and top do?' asked Sophie.

'Oh, that'll be fine. They cater for all age groups at these village hops and the band is pretty versatile too. It's just something to cheer us up after the winter blues. There's a fish 'n' chip supper too — did Keir mention that?'

Sophie shook her head, relieved that she didn't have to go dashing off to buy a more glamorous outfit. She had felt tempted to confide in Crystal about what Keir had said concerning Hugh and the craft centre, but something prevented her.

'You're seeing quite a bit of Keir, aren't you?' Crystal remarked.

'Not so much as you're seeing of Alan,' Sophie rejoined with a little laugh.

The colour tinged Crystal's cheeks. 'Yes, we do seem to be hitting it off pretty well. Alan's first wife died a few years ago. He's so much more mature than the other guys I've dated and we've lots in common.'

'That's good. I think Keir's just being nice to me because he's Aunt Rose's neighbour. I'm sure our paths wouldn't have crossed otherwise,' Sophie said lightly. 'I expect he's got someone tucked away somewhere.'

'Mum says he's a bit of a man of mystery. Nobody seems to know much about him, although he's certainly making his presence felt in Penbridge.'

'He's obviously a friend of Erica's,' Sophie said carefully. 'I mean she's rented him the house lock, stock and barrel so she must trust him.'

'Oh, yes, she does that all right. It seems they used to live near each other at one time — Gloucestershire, Worcestershire — that area. We all think he's nursing a broken heart. Some woman's thrown him over. Either that or he's someone famous in hiding.'

'Crystal, you've been reading far too many library books! Actually, he did tell me he fancied a change of environment. Periodically everyone needs to take time out to recharge their batteries. Although, it seems he's got a pretty busy life for someone who's doing that.'

'Mmm, he's a brilliant teacher. I really enjoyed the class last week. Now that you're staying around for a bit you ought to see if you can join. They're a friendly crowd, although Glenda can be a bit tiresome, always wanting Keir's attention. Between you and me, I think she deliberately makes a mess of what she's doing so that he'll come and sort it out.'

'Surely the intelligent thing to do would be to make such a good job of it that she won his admiration.'

'I know what to expect from you then,' Crystal teased. 'You'll turn out to be top of the class.'

'I very much doubt that!' Sophie protested. 'I know virtually nothing about ceramics, although I'd certainly like to give it a go. Maybe I'll have a word with Keir.'

Sophie knew she'd enjoy every minute she spent with Keir, providing she didn't allow herself to think about what had really brought him to Penbridge. Was he recovering from a broken relationship the same as herself?

'Well, as I've said before it'll be interesting to see what happens when Erica returns. Will she sell up to Keir or . . . ' Crystal trailed off as the back door opened and her mother came into the kitchen. Sophie hoped that Erica was going to remain in Spain for some considerable time. She didn't want to think about Rowanbank without Keir.

*  *  *

'You look very nice dear,' Aunt Rose said as Sophie came into the room on Saturday night.

'I don't have too much with me, but black can always be teamed with anything.'

'And that red top looks just right. I like what you've done with your hair too and those earrings add the finishing touch.'

Sophie hoped Keir thought so too. She didn't want to look over-dressed, as she'd said to Crystal, but it wasn't always easy to get things right. The skirt was one of those useful ones that came in handy for school functions because it didn't date. Shoes were a bit of a problem so she decided to take the safe option, wear her boots and change into her shoes when they got there. Keir had said he'd pick her up at seven-thirtyish and she was ready and waiting when he arrived. It was too dark to see what he was wearing, but she could smell his distinctive cologne as she sat beside him during the short drive.

For his part, Keir was very conscious of Sophie and caught the light, floral fragrance she was wearing. He was aware of the chemistry between them and wondered if she sensed it too. He'd had absolutely no intention of becoming involved with anyone again.

One all consuming love was all he'd expected during his lifetime.

At the village hall, Sophie quickly divested herself of her coat and changed into her pumps.

Keir was waiting for her, looking elegant in his smart casual attire — a pale-blue, open-necked shirt beneath a darker blue jacket and trousers. He stood looking at her for a long moment and she felt herself colour beneath his gaze.

'Wow! Sophie, I scarcely recognise you! I wondered what you'd look like when you were really dressed up and you've swept me off my feet.'

She coloured. 'You don't look so bad yourself.'

The village hall was crowded that evening, but Crystal and Alan spotted them and beckoned them across to their table.

'Hi! We came early to help set up the hall. Doesn't it look great?'

'Certainly does, and what an excellent turnout.'

'It's always a popular event, that's why we've grabbed a table.'

Sophie had wondered how the dancing would be organised with such a small dance floor, but it all worked beautifully. As Crystal had said, there was something for every age group and taste.

It was all very informal and great fun. After they'd watched Crystal being twirled about the hall by Alan, who was surprisingly nimble on his feet, Keir stood up and caught Sophie's hand.

'Come on, let's show them what we're made of!'

He whirled her away as the band struck up a popular number. Laughingly, she followed his lead. It seemed that most people seemed to put their own interpretation to the music if they didn't know the steps, and Keir was no exception. Not for the first time, Sophie noted that, for a fairly large man, he was agile and moved rhythmically. She was a reasonably good dancer herself and enjoyed matching his steps and experiencing a thrill of pleasure at being in his company. After a time, he caught her hand and they went into a side room for a breather.

'That was fun!' she told him breathlessly, cheeks flushed.

'I thought so too. Didn't we do well!' He leant towards her, a purposeful gleam in his eyes and she felt her heart hammering, anticipating his kiss.

'So this is where you're hiding, Keir!' Glenda appeared as if from thin air. She was wearing a tight-fitting, short red dress with a plunging neckline.

'Come on, you promised me a dance,

'remember?' and she led him meekly away.

'That girl is unbelievable,' Crystal said, as Sophie rejoined them feeling completely deflated. 'She came with a group of friends, but she's intent on monopolising Keir's attention.'

'Well, he doesn't appear to object.' Sophie said shortly, watching the pair of them.

Crystal shrugged. 'Oh, Keir's one of those lovely men who's able to make any woman feel she's the centre of his universe when she's with him.'

A remark which only served to make Sophie feel even more miserable. Why had he asked her to be his partner if he'd known Glenda was going to be there?

Glenda was gyrating to the music in the most amazing way and Sophie thought she was deliberately showing off.

After a while, Keir laughingly excused himself and returned to the table.

'That was a little too energetic for

me,' he said mopping his brow, 'but hopefully I've shed a pound or two.'

'Well, you certainly seemed to be enjoying yourself,' Sophie remarked tartly, before she could prevent herself, and lowered her gaze as she caught the surprised look he shot at her. After all, she supposed he'd only asked her out of courtesy, because she was staying with his neighbour. It wouldn't do to get too involved with a man whom she might never see again once she'd left Penbridge. Even as she thought this, she realised it was too late.

She was involved with him emotionally and she only had herself to blame for allowing a situation to grow which could only lead to her getting hurt all over again.

'I didn't realise Glenda worked at your school,' Crystal said, to cover an awkward moment.

'Yes, she's one of the clerical assistants, but she's also a friend of Beverley who works in my department. Beverley and her husband, Pete, who's my boss, are an extremely hospitable couple and have invited me over to their place several times since I've moved here.'

*And no doubt, Glenda had been there as well,* Sophie thought dully. So much for her thinking that Glenda was just one of Keir's students. He obviously knew her socially too.

Fortunately, supper and the raffle followed and, during the general banter and camaraderie there was no time to dwell on the incident. If Sophie could have only known it, Keir was kicking himself for not handling the situation better. He was all too aware that Glenda could be a bit manipulative.

She was a lively girl, who was the life and soul of the party but, at times, he found her a little wearing and immature.

The dancing continued after supper, but when Alan and Crystal got up to leave, Keir and Sophie followed suit.

'That was a pleasant evening,' Keir remarked on the drive home. 'I hope you've enjoyed it too.'

'Absolutely! It's good to support local events. Thanks for asking me,' she said, trying to keep her voice steady.

'I enjoy your company, Sophie. Have you thought any more about joining my ceramics class?'

She hesitated a moment, wondering if she could tolerate Glenda, but Crystal would be there too. She knew she'd love to spend more time in Keir's company.

'You could come for one session and see if you liked it,' he suggested.

'I'd enjoy that,' she told him sincerely.

'Good, I'll keep you to that.' He pulled up outside Rose Cottage. 'That's odd — it's in total darkness. Will Rose have gone to bed this early?'

'Probably, but she'd have left a light on. The porch light was on when I left too,' Sophie said worriedly.

'I'm sure there's a simple explanation. She probably switched it off by mistake, but just in case, I'll come in with you. I've got a torch in the glove compartment.'

Sophie was glad of Keir's support. Without any street lights, it was very dark at night and there were no lights in the neighbouring cottage either, as Ian and Fiona had obviously not yet returned from the dance.

Sophie's heart was racing as they pushed open the sitting room door and were greeted by a loud meow from Poppy and a mumble from Aunt Rose.

Keir shone the torch and Rose looked up dazedly.

'Oh, my goodness, you did give me a start! Whatever time is it?'

'About eleven. Why are you sitting in the dark?' asked Sophie, fumbling around for the light switch.

She flicked it on but nothing happened.

'There was a flash and all the lights went out. I decided it was best to stay put until you came in. I expect it's that thingummyjig they fitted when they did the electrical work a couple of years

163

back. I never could get the hang of it. Hugh always saw to it for me.'

'Do you mean the trip switch?' asked Keir. 'I'll sort it out in a jiffy if you tell me where the box is. You sit tight. Sophie, can you come with me and be my official torch bearer?'

Five minutes later the problem was resolved, much to Aunt Rose's relief.

'You're freezing cold,' Sophie said, rubbing Rose's hands.

'I'd just turned the fire off and I didn't attempt to turn it on again, just in case something else blew up,' Aunt Rose said, looking sheepish.

'Never mind, problem solved. I think your light bulb must have blown,' Keir told her. 'I'll sort it out in the morning. For now we'll make do with the side lamp and some hot drinks.'

Sophie shot into the dining room and returned with a travel rug from Aunt Rose's bed and draped it over her knees, in spite of her protests.

\* \* \*

'I worry about Rose,' Keir said, as they stood in the kitchen waiting for the kettle to boil. 'If you hadn't been staying here, she would have probably remained like that until the morning.'

'I'm just relieved you were here and, now that you've shown me what to do, I'll sort it, if it happens again. Now, just remind me how you like your coffee.'

'Before I do, Miss Burnett, I'd like to thank you for your company this evening,' he said quietly and, before she'd realised it, he'd caught her round the waist and pulled her to him.

'Your hair smells of flowers,' he murmured and kissed her lightly on the mouth, and then as she responded, more passionately, kindling a flame of desire within her. Just as suddenly, he released her, leaving her feeling as if she'd been on a roller coaster.

'That kettle's boiling,' he announced, as if nothing had happened, and making the drinks, he carried the tray into the sitting room.

She knew she oughtn't to read too

much into that kiss. It had just been a thank you for the evening, but he had left her in no doubt as to her feelings for him.

Her emotions were in turmoil and she wanted to believe that the chemistry she'd sensed between them was real and not a figment of her imagination.

As Sophie showed Keir out into the inky blackness of the night, she said shyly, 'Thanks for a lovely evening, Keir.'

He took her hands between his for a minute. 'The pleasure was all mine,' he said softly and disappeared out into the night smiling to himself. He suddenly felt life was worth living again, and it was all thanks to Sophie Burnett.

# A New Job

'I've got a bit of a problem, Sophie,' Aunt Rose told her the following morning over breakfast. 'We had enough to think about last night, so I didn't mention it then.'

Sophie buttered a slice of toast. 'What's wrong, is your ankle playing up?'

'No, dear, it's nothing like that. The thing is, it's Mary's birthday next Saturday. Hugh and I always bought flowers and took them to the church yard but . . . '

'Well, that's OK. I'll take you to choose some and we'll go together.'

'Would you, dear. That would be nice — except . . . '

Something suddenly registered. 'Wait a minute, if it was Aunt Mary's birthday then it's obviously got to be yours as well, hasn't it?'

Rose nodded. 'Daphne rang up last

night. She wants to know if she can come and see me on Saturday and bring little Lily. Apparently Daphne's husband, Neil, is working in the morning.'

'OK, well that's no problem. I can make myself scarce so that you can have some quality time with Daphne and Lily,' Sophie assured her.

'Oh no, dear, you're part of my extended family and I don't intend to exclude you. I'll just have to think round it. Daphne's always in a rush. I doubt if she'll stay to tea and, if I want to go to the churchyard first and cook lunch, it'll be a bit of a tight squeeze. I was wondering about roast chicken. Anyway, I'll phone Daphne again later in the week. She's always so vague about timing, says she's got to do some shopping first at the designer outlet. Apparently, they're going skiing in February when it's Lily's half term.'

Unbeknown to them over at Rowan-bank, Keir was facing the same kind of dilemma.

One of Hugh's requests, left with his will, was that flowers be placed on Mary's grave periodically, but particularly on her birthday and the anniversary of her death.

Erica wasn't very good at that sort of thing, saying that she found graveyards creepy places and wasn't into all that sentimental stuff. Keir wondered if he should ask Rose Harding if she wanted to accompany him, but realised it was her birthday too. No, he'd just have to do what he thought was right.

He turned his thoughts to other matters. Things were going smoothly with the craft centre project and targets were being met. The two people who had sparked all this off would have been ecstatic, had they been alive to see it.

Erica had given Keir carte blanche to do whatever he thought was best. Just so long as she didn't have to concern herself with it, she didn't seem to care. If only he could win Rose over, but that was proving more difficult. The phone rang and he snatched it up.

'Keir, you really are proving quite elusive to get hold of these days,' came Erica's voice.

'And you haven't replied to my last two e-mails. It really is too bad of you! I am allowed a social life, as well as you,' Keir told her, a trifle impatiently. 'So what can I do for you?'

Keir put the phone down and sat staring into space. Sometimes Erica could be quite infuriating. He'd discovered she was very good at delegating and, somehow she always managed to get him to agree to do her bidding. This time it was some correspondence she wanted him to deal with on her behalf.

During the week, Sophie helped Aunt Rose move back upstairs so that the dining room could be made ready for the visitors on Saturday. Sophie took Rose into Tonbridge for a supermarket shop and they returned laden with groceries. It would have been so much easier if Daphne had offered to take Aunt Rose out for lunch, but that obviously wasn't her style.

It was towards the end of the week before Sophie saw Keir again. He had offered to give her a lift to his evening class. She was feeling apprehensive on several counts, not least of them being because she didn't want to look foolish in front of Keir and the others, if she couldn't master what she was asked to do.

She needn't have worried because Keir set her to work making pinch pots whilst the rest of the class continued with their previous week's task. After this they all attempted some jewellery which was fiddly and would need to be biscuit fired to a very high temperature.

'Told you you'd enjoy it,' Crystal said, as she bent over the earrings she was making.

'How are you getting on?' Keir enquired, examining the geometric shapes Sophie was endeavouring to cut from the porcelain clay. 'You know I can't believe you're a beginner.'

She coloured, so aware of him standing

beside her that she was unable to concentrate.

'Well, actually, I used to help out in an after school club when they needed an extra pair of hands, but someone else was in charge,' she confessed.

His eyes glinted. 'And all this time you've been telling me you know next to nothing about ceramics!'

'I don't at this level, but I can make pinch and coil pots, although they're a bit lop-sided, as you can see. I've never tried my hand at anything as ambitious as the jewellery before.'

During the coffee break Glenda came to speak to Sophie. 'This is supposed to be a beginners' class,' she stated.

'Yes, I realise that. I am a beginner.'

'You can hardly be a novice if you've supported children in pottery classes, as I heard you telling Keir.'

'That doesn't really count,' Sophie assured her. 'Call it beginner's luck, if you like. It'll probably all break in the kiln.'

Crystal overhearing this, came to the

rescue. 'Sophie's a teacher so she's probably tried her hand at a number of things, isn't that right, Sophie?'

Sophie nodded, thankful for the interruption. 'You know that saying, Jack of all trades, master of none? Well, that's me.'

Fortunately just then, someone else claimed Glenda's attention.

'What is wrong with that girl?' Crystal murmured. 'Keir's perfectly fair to everyone, but for some reason, she must be stage centre.'

At the end of the class, Glenda did her utmost to detain Keir, but he laughingly told her that he needed to lock up. When she realised he was giving Sophie a lift home, she soon made herself scarce.

'So, Sophie, what did you think?' Keir asked during the short drive home.

'I enjoyed myself. Thanks for inviting me.'

'You're very welcome, but the pleasure's all mine,' he assured her. 'I can already see you've got talent.'

Sophie felt a warm glow at his unexpected praise.

It was a glorious morning on Saturday. Aunt Rose was up early. Over breakfast she opened her presents and cards, expressing delight at the cardigan Sophie's family had sent her and the pretty little brooch Sophie had purchased from Peggy Munn's.

Before they set out for the churchyard, the vegetables were prepared and the chicken was put in the oven. They'd managed to buy some rather nice flowers at the farm shop. It didn't take long to accomplish their mission, but they were surprised to see someone had been there before them. Aunt Rose looked at Sophie in surprise.

As they retraced their steps they spotted Keir on a bench looking out over the tranquil view. Sophie thought he looked a bit pensive.

'Good morning, ladies. I expect you've just been to the same place as myself.'

'But how did you know about today?' Aunt Rose asked, mystified.

'Hugh left several instructions with his will,' Keir explained briefly, 'and as Erica's not around to see that they're carried out, I've volunteered. Now I understand it's your birthday too, Rose, and so I was wondering if I could take the pair of you out to lunch?'

Rose looked disappointed. 'Oh, Keir, what a charming thought, but I've got Tom's niece, Daphne, coming with her little girl — just for their usual flying visit. Tell you what though — why don't you join us? There's a chicken roasting in the oven so there'll be plenty of food.'

'Oh, I wouldn't want to intrude if you've got guests . . . '

'That's what Sophie said, but it'd be more like a party then. We'll be eating around one o'clock and you're more than welcome. Please do come.'

To Sophie's secret delight Keir agreed and they went their separate ways. Daphne and Lily arrived just before one o'clock. Lily was clutching a strangely shaped package and Daphne handed Rose an expensive looking, gift-wrapped box of chocolates.

Lily looked anxiously at Aunt Rose as that lady unwrapped her gift to reveal the most unbelievably ugly jam pot Sophie had ever seen, in bright garish colours with a large bee perched on the top.

'I choosed it myself,' Lily informed her, proudly.

'Chose, darling,' Daphne corrected automatically.

'It's quite — quite fabulous,' Aunt Rose told her. 'I've never seen anything like this one before.'

Sophie, biting her lip, had a feeling that even Peggy Munn would have been hard-pressed to accommodate it.

At one o'clock, Keir arrived and, shortly afterwards, they all sat down to lunch. Daphne monopolised the conversation, as Sophie seemed to remember she always did. Keir was his usual charming self and Aunt Rose was obviously enjoying having people around her to celebrate her birthday.

Daphne asked Keir about his job and spent a while outlining hers, as PA to the director of a leading brand of cosmetics. She then turned to Sophie.

'So what are your plans for the future? Have you got another job lined up?'

Sophie shook her head catching Keir's interested gaze. 'Not at present, no. I've been taking a break for a few weeks.'

'So does that mean you'll eventually be returning to Hertfordshire?'

Keir was watching Sophie intently. 'Probably not — I rather like it here in Kent,' she said with a smile and got up to clear away the dishes, aware that Daphne was giving her a hard look. Surely she didn't object to Sophie staying at Rose Cottage?

'So, Keir,' Daphne said, as they ate a rather gooey dessert made especially for Lily's benefit. 'Have you come across those heirlooms that were supposed to be left to Aunt Rose and Sophie's parents?'

Aunt Rose shot her a warning glance, and Sophie was indignant that Daphne should mention this today of all days. Keir shook his head.

'I am aware of it from Erica, of course, but it's all a bit of a mystery,' he said, helping himself to the cream.

'My dad says I'm good at solving mysteries,' Lily piped up. 'I'm going to be a detective when I grow up.'

'That's nice, dear,' Aunt Rose said, a twinkle in her eye. 'Then you'll be able to find all the lost things in my house. I'm always mislaying my scissors and my glasses and sometimes even the cat.'

The little girl giggled and Daphne said rather sharply, 'Stop talking and eat your dessert, Lily'

Lily obediently did so and then, setting down her spoon asked, 'Is Amy coming over this afternoon, Aunty Rose?'

Before Rose could reply Daphne said, 'There won't be time, Lily. I've already told you, Daddy and I are going out this evening, so we need to leave here quite early before the traffic builds up on the motorway.'

'But Amy texted me. She's at her grandma's today and her Aunt Crystal's got rabbits. She said I could see them.'

'Oh, that'll keep for another day,' Daphne said impatiently, 'besides, you've got your best clothes on and you might get dirty.'

The child looked crestfallen.

'I could run Lily to the Briggs after lunch, just for a short time,' Keir offered. 'I'm sure Sophie would come with me and then you and Rose can spend some quality time together.'

'What a good idea,' Sophie enthused. 'Now, if your mum agrees, what can I find you to wear, Lily? Oh, I know, you can put one of my sweatshirts over your clothes to keep them clean.'

'Oh, please, Mummy, just for a little while,' Lily begged.

'OK, but I'm leaving around four-thirty or we'll never get back home,'

Daphne told her, not looking at all pleased, but also not wanting to lose face in front of the others, Sophie suspected.

They spent a delightful hour at the Briggs. Crystal took the the girls off to see the rabbits and Keir and Sophie opted to come as well. Afterwards, whilst the two girls were enjoying some catch-up time, Mrs Briggs insisted on making tea and produced one of her famous fruit cakes which Keir and Sophie had to sample in spite of still being full from lunch.

Mr Briggs showed Keir a large urn-shaped vase he'd inherited from his grandmother and seemed pleased when Keir informed him it was probably worth at least a hundred pounds. The two men then became engrossed in a conversation about sport.

'I wonder where those two lassies have got to?' Mavis asked a little later.

She went in search of them and Crystal came to sit beside Sophie.

'Alan's taking me to see a film this

evening. I hadn't realised it was Mrs Harding's birthday today or I'd have given her a card, but Mum's going to send her one of her cakes. Daphne's paying one of her rare visits then?'

Sophie nodded. 'She and Aunt Rose are having a chat. Keir offered to take Aunt Rose out to lunch, but he came to us instead.'

'Lily's a lovely child. She and Amy get on really well, when they do get to see each other; both being only children. It's just a pity Daphne seems to forget Lily needs to play.'

\*   \*   \*

'Well, that was a pleasant little interlude,' Keir remarked on the short journey home. 'Those are fine rabbits Crystal's got, aren't they, Lily?'

'Yes, I'm going to ask Mummy if I can have a rabbit, but she'll say no. She doesn't like pets — says they make a mess.'

Sophie felt sorry for the little girl

whose mother cared more about her appearance than letting her have any fun.

Aunt Rose and Daphne were finishing cups of tea when they arrived back. Daphne got to her feet. 'Right, we'd best be on our way. Come on Lily, get yourself tidied up and thank Aunt Rose for our lunch.'

'You're very welcome, lovey,' Rose told Lily, as the child said her piece and then stood struggling to remove the sweatshirt until Sophie came to her rescue.

Keir and Sophie left Rose to say her goodbyes.

Keir picked up his coat. 'Regretfully, I must be making tracks too, I'm going out again this evening.'

With Glenda? Sophie wondered, feeling a sudden prickle of jealousy.

When Aunt Rose returned to the sitting room, Keir produced a parcel from a bag which he'd brought in from the car.

'Sorry it's not wrapped too specially, but I thought you might like to have this.'

'Keir, there's really was no need! Your company was sufficient.'

Aunt Rose unwrapped the package carefully and gasped in delight at the delicate ceramic bowl.

'That was Hugh and Mary's! I can see it now, standing on their sideboard full of pot pourri. I'd forgotten about it until this moment, Keir. Are you sure you can bear to part with it?'

'I wouldn't be giving it to you if I couldn't,' he said with a smile at the look of sheer delight on the elderly lady's face. 'I know that you'll cherish it. I also know that Hugh promised you a keep-sake and, as it hasn't turned up and no-one seems to have any idea of what it might have been, I thought you might like this. Of course, if you would rather have the money I could arrange to sell this for you, but I'm afraid it isn't that valuable.'

'Oh, no, Keir, I wouldn't dream of it. I just love this bowl and I'll never part with it. Thank you so much!' And she kissed his cheek.

The contrast between the bowl and the jam pot was marked, but both had been given with a lot of thought, and it was the thought that counted, after all, Sophie reflected. Uncle Hugh must have thought a great deal of Keir, to have left him his entire collection of ceramics. She wondered about the identity of the potter whose work they'd both been so keen on. She sensed there was a story here.

When Keir had gone, Aunt Rose studied the bowl, turning it this way and that.

'This is such a wonderful surprise. I quite thought Erica would have got rid of it long ago, but if it was left to Keir then she couldn't. What a lovely day I've had!'

★   ★   ★

Sophie's parents rang that evening and, after speaking to Rose, had a chat with Sophie.

'Rose was telling me about the bowl

her neighbour's given her, that had belonged to Hugh. That was a nice gesture. It's all a bit puzzling though, isn't it?' her father said.

'I suppose so, but I think you'll just have to accept that you're not going to inherit the crown jewels or even a Ming vase!'

Her father laughed. 'Now, changing the subject, is there any prospect of you finding any work down in Penbridge?'

'I haven't started looking yet, but I'm going to shortly,' she told him. 'In fact I was thinking of enrolling at one of the agencies next week. I'm sure something will crop up, although it may have to be learning support work to begin with.'

After she'd put the phone down, Sophie sat staring into space. If the truth were known, she was happy here in Penbridge. She loved having time to herself and she wasn't at all sure that she wanted to take on another permanent teaching post just yet.

She knew that she was becoming increasingly attached to Keir, and loved the feeling that he was only living a short distance away from Rose Cottage. Memories of Brett were gradually beginning to fade like a bad dream, and she was looking forward to each day again.

On Monday evening, Sophie received a surprise phone call from Keir.

'Am I right in thinking you might be interested in taking on some work round here?' he asked without pre-amble.

'Well, yes. I'm going to start ringing round the agencies,' she told him, startled.

'I think I might have come up with a short term solution, if it would help. Look, can you come over to Rowan-bank in about an hour? I've got a bit of preparation to polish off first.'

Curiouser and curiouser, Sophie thought, as she walked the short distance to Rowanbank, swinging her torch. Keir showed her into the sitting room.

'I'm afraid the study's full of papers

and books,' he apologised. 'Why are you laughing?'

'Well, studies usually are, aren't they?' she chuckled.

'What, oh!' He laughed too. 'I've just made some coffee. Would you like some?'

He poured the coffee and leant back in his chair. 'The thing is, Sophie, one of the learning support assistants at the school I'm working at has been rushed into hospital with a rather nasty knee injury. Now, I know that learning support isn't quite the kind of work you were looking for and it's only part-time but . . . '

'Hold on — it'd have to be advertised, wouldn't it?' Sophie pointed out, determined not to appear too excited.

'Seriously, Sophie, I'm sure you'd be in with a good chance, but it's only a job share — two-and-a-half days a week, and the pay's not a fraction of what you'd be getting as a teacher — although with your experience it might be possible to negotiate a higher hourly rate.'

Sophie sipped her coffee, her mind in a whirl. 'So what subjects would it be, and what makes you think I'd be in with a chance?' she asked cautiously.

'You'd be supporting some of the younger pupils in subjects like English, maths and IT, science — oh and my classes too. Actually, I think you'd be very much in with a chance, because the Head knows you. Apparently, he used to teach in the same school as you in Buckinghamshire.'

Sophie gaped at him. 'Not Peter Standish? I'd completely forgotten he'd moved to Kent. He was one of our deputy heads.'

Keir nodded. 'His wife, Beverley, works in the Art department as I've probably mentioned. We're in a bit of a fix, Sophie, so would you be prepared to help out for a few weeks?'

Sophie's head was in a whirl. She'd had no idea Peter Standish was head of Keir's school. He was a thoroughly nice man, but they'd somehow lost touch since he'd moved away from Buckinghamshire.

'It certainly sounds too good to be true, but wouldn't there be a lot of objections to my being appointed without the usual rigmorole — always supposing Peter approved my application and I got the job?'

'Oh, I'm sure there are ways round these things — extenuating circumstances etc. So what shall I tell Peter?'

Everything was moving so quickly that Sophie felt as if her head was in a spin. Whilst she was sitting there, Keir sent an e-mail to Peter, who very shortly afterwards phoned back and arranged that she would call to see him the following morning.

The next morning Sophie got up at the crack of dawn to check through her CV.

Fortunately, she'd had several copies ready in a folder which she'd asked her mother to send via Tim, just in case. She realised that she might need to make a formal application, but at least she had something to present.

Sophie arrived at reception at the appointed time and the first person she encountered was Glenda.

'Yes?' she demanded curtly.

'I've an appointment to see Mr Standish at ten-thirty,' Sophie said politely.

To her surprise and relief, Peter Standish appeared in the entrance hall at that precise moment, talking to a distinguished looking gentleman with a sheaf of papers in his hand.

Peter raised a hand in greeting, as he spotted Sophie and, after his visitor had left, came across and shook her warmly by the hand. Glenda's eyes nearly popped out of her head.

'Sophie, how lovely to see you again! Well, this is a stroke of good luck for us! Come along to my office. We'll have an informal chat to start with and then I'll introduce you to some of the other members of the team.'

Sophie felt totally relaxed as she and Peter spent the first few minutes catching up on the past eighteen months, but then he forward in his chair, clasped his hands together and said, 'OK, Sophie, so let's get down to the nitty gritty. Why would someone with your expertise want to apply for a temporary post like this one? You were head of department in Bucks so what happened?'

Sophie coloured, but was prepared to be honest. 'I, er, got involved with someone in the area. The relationship didn't work out and so I decided it would be best to make a fresh start, so I returned to Hertfordshire to live with my parents for a time. Since then I've been doing agency work.'

Peter nodded. 'Right — well, thanks for being so honest. I understand you came to Penbridge to help out an elderly friend. Are you planning to remain there for some length of time at all? Have you settled in?'

'It's a nice place and I certainly like it, so for the time being, yes.'

'OK, well we could certainly use your

expertise, and I could negotiate your hourly rate, but I'm afraid it wouldn't be anything comparable to what you have been used to receiving previously.'

They talked generally for a time and then Peter glanced at the clock and got to his feet.

'I'll introduce you to the head of Learning Support and the pastoral care person. If it was down to me you could start straight away, but you know what it's like nowadays. There are certain rules we have to observe.'

The rest of the day was so hectic that Sophie didn't have time to reflect on whether or not she'd made the right decision. Peter Standish arranged for some sixth formers to take her on a whistlestop tour of the school.

Over lunch, Sophie met the various people she would be directly involved with and then, in the afternoon, after a brief interview, she was whisked off to the English department to work with a couple of children under the supervision of another member of staff. From there she was directed to an to an IT class.

It was a totally different experience for her, taking instructions from other teachers and working alongside them, rather than being in control of things herself.

Later, as she got into her car, Sophie realised that she hadn't encountered Keir once that day. Actually, she hadn't been to the Art and Craft department yet. Her guides had merely waved their hands in the general direction.

The situation was rectified the very next morning when she realised she would be working with Keir after break and up until lunchtime.

Keir was as good a teacher as Sophie had thought he would be — friendly, but professional. The children she was working with took up most of her attention, but she was extremely aware of him and realised that he had a good rapport with his students.

At lunch time he introduced her to the rest of the department, amongst them Beverley Standish, Peter's wife, whom she had met previously, on several occasions in Buckinghamshire.

'What a small world,' Beverley said. 'You and Keir must come over for a meal one evening.'

Startled Sophie wondered if Beverley thought they were an item and knew she'd be happy if they were. Beverley walked over to the canteen with her.

'Keir's such an asset to the department,' she commented. 'He's got such a positive attitude, which is wonderful when you consider all that he's been through.'

Sophie murmured in agreement, wondering what on earth Beverley meant and not wishing to show her ignorance.

'Of course, Hugh Mercer was a school governor. He was so involved with the craft centre and it's such a pity he didn't live to see it come to fruition. Peter and I were sorry we couldn't take another look round the other Saturday, but I'm afraid other commitments overtook. As you probably remember, we've got two young children and Peter's tied up very often in the evenings, so we couldn't get to Keir's talk either, but I gather it was very good.'

'Glenda was there,' Sophie said carefully, wondering how Beverley would reply.

Beverley smiled. 'Yes, Glenda's a staunch supporter of Keir's. Her parents live a stone's throw from us — her father's another one of our governors. Anyway, as she'd recently split up from her boyfriend, we asked her along to supper back in the autumn, and Keir was there too with some of the other newly appointed members of staff. They got chatting and she became hooked on ceramics.'

It seemed Glenda had got hooked on Keir too, Sophie thought cynically. They reached the dining hall and Beverley changed the subject back to school topics and didn't mention either Keir or Glenda again.

Sophie encountered Keir in the car park, as she was about to drive home.

'You did well this morning,' he told her. 'You're already forming a rapport with the children, which is half the battle. Are you enjoying it so far?'

'Yes, although it's certainly a very different ball game from mainstream teaching,' she told him, 'but such good experience. The children are delightful.'

'And the staff?'

'Oh, those are delightful too,' she said with a little laugh. 'I had lunch with Beverley.'

'Good, she's a nice person to know, but of course, you'd met her before in Buckinghamshire. I was forgetting.'

'Oh, just at social functions, that sort of thing.' She didn't want to talk about Buckinghamshire and Keir seemed to sense this.

Glenda appeared from one of the buildings with a sheaf of papers in her hand. Spotting Keir she made a detour. 'Phew. Just caught up with you in time!' She totally ignored Sophie and handed him one of the sheets. 'More bumph, I'm afraid. You're not in tomorrow, are you?'

'Nope, but I've got enough paperwork to last me for several days.'

She fluttered her eyelashes at him. 'I'm so looking forward to your next ceramics class, Keir. What are we going to be doing?'

He laughed. 'If I told you, you'd be as wise as me — sorry Glenda you'll have to wait.'

'You're such a tease, Keir,' she told him laughingly and flounced off.

'Are you joining us this week, Sophie?' he asked.

'Oh, yes, I'm looking forward to it, but you must let me know how much I owe you.'

He mentioned a sum which seemed far too modest and, embarrassed, she wondered if he was asking her to pay less than the others.

'See you there then,' he said, before she could challenge him, and, getting into his car, drove off with a wave of his hand.

# A Rival for Keir

'Darling, that's wonderful news,' her mother said when Sophie rang her that evening to tell her about the job. 'You never know what else it might lead to either.'

'I only started properly today,' Sophie pointed out. 'It's only a very temporary job. It's an amazing coincidence running into Peter Standish like that.'

'Does he know about Brett?' her mother asked.

Sophie swallowed. 'I obviously had to tell Peter my reasons for leaving my post, particularly as he's still in touch with several people in Bucks. It simply wouldn't do to be economical with the truth or it might jeopardise any future prospects of work.'

After the phone call, Sophie sat deep in thought. Some days she believed she was over Brett, but then something sparked off a memory and it was as if it was only yesterday when they'd parted company. Her thoughts turned to Keir. He was so completely different from Brett — far more mature for one thing and he certainly attracted her, but she still wondered if he was harbouring some lost love and knew she couldn't bear to get hurt all over again.

'Sophie, can you spare a minute?' Aunt Rose called and she went into the sitting room to find Rose needed a hand with some of the more fiddly dolls' house furnishings.

'My hands are really playing up today. I suppose the time will come when I'll have to call a halt to all this. Your mother asked me if she could bring your grandmother for a visit soon. It must be donkey's years since I last saw Beryl.'

'She's about the same as ever,' Sophie said with a little smile. 'Does very well for her age. Apparently she's reorganising Mum's kitchen cupboards. Mum doesn't mind if it keeps her occupied.'

'Well, she can reorganise mine any day,' laughed Rose. 'Now, dear, if you could just hold this whilst I glue on the material. It's a good job I'm not on piece work or I'd get the sack!'

After a time Sophie said, 'Aunt Rose — someone mentioned that Keir had been through a difficult time before he moved here. She obviously assumed I knew what she meant, but I didn't know what she was talking about.'

Aunt Rose gave her a shrewd look from her bright blue eyes. 'And I don't either, dear. I suspect that he's come here to get away from past experiences, the same as you have, and that if he wants to confide in you then he will, don't you?'

Sophie opened her mouth to make some comment, but decided against it. She was curious about Keir, but sometimes ignorance was bliss and, after all, she couldn't expect him to unburden himself to her, not unless she was prepared to reciprocate and tell him about Brett, and she knew she still wasn't quite ready for that.

After a few minutes, Aunt Rose said, 'I should be helping Peggy in the shop tomorrow, but her nephew's rung to say she's got a cold. His wife's covering in the morning but can't manage the afternoon, and I really don't feel like being there on my own all that time.'

'That's OK, I could lend a hand. I'm only working in the morning so I could easily pick you up for two o'clock.'

Aunt Rose visibly brightened. 'Would you, dear? That would be lovely. It gets me out of the house and if Peggy's not there, then maybe you and I could do a little more spring cleaning. Now, do you fancy a nice cup of tea?'

The following morning fairly flew past. Sophie was kept incredibly busy. The maths teacher was a peppery gentleman nearing retirement, who obviously didn't see the need for her to be there at all, and seemed to find her presence a hindrance rather than a help.

Sophie had never found maths a

particularly easy subject herself, and felt sympathy for the little girl she was working with, who simply couldn't get the hang of what she was being asked to do at all.

The lesson over-ran by several minutes and Sophie made a thankful exit nearly cannoning into Beverley in the corridor.

'I see you've met our Stanley! His bark's worse than his bite.'

Sophie grimaced. 'You don't say! Oh, well never mind, I'll get used to him, I suppose.'

Beverley chuckled. 'Every school has a Stanley. From what I gather, you're doing brilliantly, so don't let him get you down. Now, how about you coming for that meal on Saturday evening? Keir's free, if you are. I realise it's short notice, but my parents are taking the children to Chessington Zoo and Adventure Park, and keeping them overnight. We'd actually have a child-free zone, and that's rare. So what do you say?'

'I'd love to come, thanks a lot,' she said warmly.

'Great! I'll look forward to seeing you around sevenish. I'm sure Keir will liaise with you over transport, but just in case . . . ' She rummaged in her bag and handed Sophie an address sticker.

Suddenly Sophie realised Glenda had appeared and was hovering by Beverley's side.

'Hello Glenda, did you want to see me about something?'

'Yes, if I might have a word, Bev,' she said, and Sophie wondered how long Glenda had been standing there.

'Of course, bye then Sophie — see you soon.'

# An Interesting Discovery

It was a hectic afternoon because Aunt Rose and Sophie took advantage of Peggy's absence to do a bit of spring cleaning, making sure to replace items where they had been before.

'My goodness that looks better,' Aunt Rose said in a satisfied voice. 'You can actually see the colour of that china. I'm surprised Peggy hasn't appeared to see what we're up to.'

Halfway through the afternoon, Rose took the elderly lady some tea.

'That cold has really taken its toll on her. She looks worn out, poor thing!'

Soon afterwards, the door opened and Crystal and Amy came into the shop.

'Amy's off to a party tomorrow and, as her mum's working, I said we'd try to find a present for her friend.'

Amy wandered contentedly round

the shop, with Aunt Rose keeping a discreet eye on her. Eventually, the little girl returned to the counter clutching a pottery rabbit.

'She'd like that. It's just like one of Aunt Crystal's rabbits.'

'Are you sure it's not you that likes it?' Crystal enquired. 'I don't actually remember Zoe coming to see my rabbits.'

'No, but if she did she'd like them,' Amy persisted.

'OK, but perhaps you should give it to her with an invitation to come to see the real thing?' Crystal told her and winked at Aunt Rose, who took Amy's money and found her a box for the rabbit. Crystal picked up an attractive notepad, ruler and pencil set with the name Zoe emblazoned on it.

'We'll add this as well,' she said, 'I must say this shop's looking very spick and span. I hardly recognise it. I can actually see my face in that counter and there's not a designer cobweb in sight and as for that window display, it's a credit to you and Keir, Sophie!'

'Well, we've all done our best,' Aunt Rose said. 'We're making one last ditch effort to save this shop from going under. Just because there's a fancy place on its way to opening, why should we be pushed out?'

Fortunately, Crystal was saved from replying when a couple of mums appeared with their children in tow. Crystal exchanged a meaningful look with Sophie, before leaving the shop.

Keir's class was even more enjoyable than the week before. First they were shown how to dip the biscuit-fired earrings, cufflinks and brooches they had made the week before in a matt porcelain glaze. They then dipped the items in a stain of their choice, before placing them on newspaper.

'Next comes the tedious part,' Keir informed them. 'We have to remove the glaze from beneath the jewellery and get rid of any residue before firing again.'

The next task the class were given

was to decorate quarry tiles. Some of the group had brought their own sketches to work from whilst others selected drawings to copy.

'Pleased you came?' Crystal asked during the break.

'Absolutely, I'm really enjoying myself.'

Keir looked up with a smile. That's what I like to hear. I like to have a happy band of students. What's up, Glenda?'

'I'm not sure about this design, Keir. Come and give me your opinion.'

But Keir, merely smiled and said, 'I think you're trying to make things too complicated. Take a break and come back to it. If you're still unsure, have a look through some of those books on the table and choose something else. Sophie here has picked a very simple design and, sometimes, that's a safer bet.'

With a bad grace, Glenda took a quick look at Sophie's effort.

'Oh, I couldn't possibly do anything like that! It's far too traditional!' she exclaimed. 'I really do need your input, Keir.'

She clutched Keir's sleeve and fluttered her eyelashes at him beguilingly.

As they moved out of earshot Crystal shook her head and said incredulously, 'Whatever is she like?'

Sophie had an uncomfortable feeling that Glenda would make a bad enemy and could have wished that Keir hadn't drawn attention to her work like that.

To Rose's complete surprise, Fiona and Ian invited her round for supper on Saturday evening as Fiona's mother had come to stay for a few days. Ian arranged to collect Rose and bring her home.

'It's about time we got to know each other,' Fiona said, when she encountered Sophie in the baker's on Saturday morning. 'You'd have been welcome too, but I gather you're already going out.'

Keir phoned and arranged to pick Sophie up at six-thirty.

'It's pointless both of us taking our cars. Anyway, I don't suppose you know that neck of the woods. It's a new housing development a couple of miles out of the village.'

Sophie deliberated over what to wear and, in the end, decided on a mid-length indigo blue skirt and an embroidered tunic top. She added dangling silver earrings, made up carefully, brushed her shining hair and caught it back with a couple of glittery combs, and sprayed on a light perfume. As the door bell peeled she snatched up her coat.

Her heart leapt as Keir caught her arm and steered her towards the car.

'We're in for a pleasant evening. Beverley's an excellent cook and they're both good company.'

'Will anyone else be there?'

'Oh, I'm not sure. They're an extremely hospitable couple, as I've said before. We'll just have to wait and see, won't we?'

Beverley and Peter's house on the

outskirts of Penbridge was bright and comfortable with one or two clever touches that reflected Beverley's creativity. It seemed it was just to be the four of them. Over a delightful meal of beef casserole, they talked about general things, but suddenly during a lull in the conversation Beverley asked, 'So are you still in touch with any of the Bucks crowd, Sophie?'

'I, er, just one or two people in the English department,' she said, aware that Keir was looking at her and realising Peter wouldn't have breached her confidentiality about her reasons for leaving the school.

'Sophie's like me, always full of good intentions about keeping in touch but, once you've moved on, somehow the months just slip by,' Peter told his wife.

Over dessert the conversation inevitably turned to the craft centre.

'So are things going to schedule, Keir?' Peter asked.

'More or less. You know what builders are like, but on the whole there haven't been too many hitches.'

'What do you reckon to it, Sophie?' Beverley asked. 'Pretty amazing, isn't it?'

'Well, yes. It's certainly very enterprising,' Sophie said.

'Sophie's had her reservations,' Keir told them. 'She's worried for Peggy and Rose.'

'Oh, but surely you don't need to be. I mean that's a delightful little shop, but they could still find an outlet at the craft centre when it opens, if they wanted to move there.'

Sophie stared at Beverley. 'But they wouldn't want to. Could they afford the overheads? Not only that, but Peggy lives on the premises at the shop.'

'We'll just have to wait and see what happens then, won't we?' Beverley said rather dismissively. 'Anyway, it's good that the grant came through, isn't it, Keir?'

He nodded and looked a little awkward, probably recognising how Sophie felt about things. She hadn't really stopped to think about the funding for the craft centre and now she asked, 'Will this grant pay for all of it? It must be a very expensive project.'

Keir shook his head. 'No, but we've received a large donation from an anonymous source and we've had several fundraising events. We're also going to be in receipt of a large bequest, when it eventually comes through. Until then, we've been able to get a loan on the strength of it. It was all going ahead before Hugh died. He was the chief instigator, as I've explained.'

'I think it's a marvellous idea,' Peter said. 'When it's fully functioning, I'll bet it'll win the support of most of those who put up objections. Keir's going to give demonstrations and tuition, did he tell you, Sophie?'

'Well, no, but I haven't really had time to get my head round it all,' she told him.

They were sitting over coffee when there was a peal on the doorbell. Beverley sprang up and returned a few minutes later with Glenda.

'Look who I found on the doorstep,' she said.

'Oh, I hadn't realised you'd got company,' Glenda said innocently. 'I've just brought this catalogue for Beverley.'

'Come and sit down for a few minutes,' Peter invited. 'It looks as if its raining cats and dogs out there.'

'It is — just for a few minutes then,' She made for the sofa where Keir was sitting.

'Would you like some coffee or there's wine.'

Glenda brightened. 'Ooh wine, please.'

'So you're not out on the town with your friends tonight then?' Peter enquired.

'No, my father's invited some people round, so I've been helping my mother with dinner. They're talking politics so I decided to escape for a while and leave them to it.'

'Glenda's father is a local councillor as well as a school governor,' Keir explained to Sophie.

'Really, he leads a busy life then,' Sophie said, wondering if Glenda had realised Keir would be there that evening, and had deliberately gate-crashed the dinner party.

'He certainly does.' She smiled at Keir. 'I can't wait to see how our ceramics have turned out.'

'You're going to have to be patient, I'm afraid,' Keir told her with a pleasant smile. 'Did you know Peter and Sophie used to work together in a previous school? Small world isn't it?'

Glenda was silent for a moment, and then she said, 'My father was a little surprised when he realised she'd been taken on so quickly in Irene's place.'

'Ah well, life's full of surprises,' Peter said quickly to cover an awkward moment.

'I bet the pair of you could tell a few stories about each other then,' Glenda said undaunted.

'Only pleasant ones where Sophie is

concerned. She was brilliant at fund-raising for events such as Children In Need.'

'Obviously takes after Hugh then,' Keir commented.

'Speaking of Hugh, have you heard anything from Erica recently?' Beverley enquired.

It was Keir's turn to look startled. 'She e-mails from time to time and seems to be enjoying life in Spain. When she gets bored she'll return to England, no doubt.'

Sophie realised that she wasn't the only one waiting on his reply. Glenda's green eyes narrowed as she said, 'So when she returns to England will she come back to Penbridge?'

'I really have no idea,' Keir said shortly. 'We'll have to wait and see, won't we?'

Beverley was studying her nails and obviously wishing that she hadn't mentioned Erica and Sophie wondered again just what the connection was between Keir and Hugh's young widow.

'We were talking about the craft centre before you arrived,' Beverley said brightly.

'Oh, really. I can't wait for it to get off the ground. Of course, my father thinks it's all a bit frivolous. He's a bit peeved that it's all going ahead.'

'Perhaps he'll change his mind once it's opened,' Keir said.

'You don't know my father,' Glenda told him, helping herself to a handful of peanuts.

'But I think I do,' Peter said with a grin. 'I reckon we'll win him round eventually. Now would anyone like any more coffee?'

'Now that the quaint old shop where we've been displaying our ceramics is closed, I suppose we'll need to find another outlet,' Glenda said.

Sophie's head shot up. 'What do you mean, closed? Aunt Rose and I were only working there on Thursday afternoon.'

Glenda examined her nails which were painted a startling blue. 'There was a closed sign on the door when I went past there this afternoon. Apparently the old woman who owns it is ill.'

'You're partly right,' Keir chipped in. 'Mrs Munn is suffering from a fluey cold and so her daughter-in-law's taken her to stay with her for a few days, but as to closing on a permanent basis, well that's not going to happen for a while yet.'

'OK, but that old biddy must be way over eighty so it's high time she retired,' Glenda said rudely.

'That old biddy, as you call her, happens to be a friend of Aunt Rose's, so I'd rather you didn't talk about her like that,' Sophie said sharply.

Glenda's eyebrows shot up. 'Sorry, I'm sure. Anyway, when she goes my father will make sure the premises are sold for something a bit more upmarket.'

Sophie bit back a retort, not wishing to descend to Glenda's level and Beverley, sensing an atmosphere between the two of them said, 'Would you like to see what we've done to the spare room, Sophie? Glenda's had a look already.'

Relieved, Sophie followed her out of the room.

'You mustn't mind Glenda, Sophie. She's very outspoken — takes after her father there. Underneath all that brashness she's really rather unsure of herself.'

'Hmm, well she'll be old one day, so let's hope she develops a more sympathetic attitude. Wow, Beverley! This room is lovely.'

'Yes, we're pleased with it. You must come again when the children are here. I've really enjoyed your company. It's good you and Keir get on so well. He's such a lovely guy. I suppose you know how he came to be living in Penbridge?'

'Well, actually . . . ' Sophie began when Peter called up the stairs.

'Phone Bev. It's your mother to tell you what sort of a day the kids have had.'

With an apologetic smile, Beverley excused herself and Sophie wished the interruption hadn't been at that precise moment.

It was getting on for ten-thirty when Keir stood up to leave. Glenda begged a lift and they departed shortly afterwards. Keir dropped her off at a large detached house. He made absolutely no comment as he drove on, but Sophie couldn't help wondering what he was thinking. For her the evening had been going so well until Glenda had turned up. It was obvious that the young woman was determined to do everything in her power to get Keir to notice her. Was Keir so impervious as he made out?

As they drove back through the village Keir remarked, 'I was sorry to hear Peggy Munn was so poorly. I actually didn't want to spoil your evening by mentioning it earlier, but I saw John Munn in the pub last night and he was telling me roughly what Glenda said. The problem is, John and his wife really can't cover the shop more than they're doing already, especially when Peggy needs looking after as well.'

'Oh, dear. She wasn't at all well on Thursday, but we hoped she was getting better now. Aunt Rose will be upset. I don't think she can take it on board that Peggy might retire.'

'OK, we'll just have to think round it, won't we?' he said mysteriously.

'How do you mean?' Sophie demanded.

'There's got to be some solution for your aunt. The craft centre will be up and running by Easter if all goes according to plan, but that's not 'til April, so there's time enough to think things through. Not only that, but the rest of us are still going to continue to need an outlet for our work in the short term, as Glenda pointed out. Don't worry, Sophie. Just because things are looking bleak at the moment, it doesn't mean to say we can't work round it. Rose's dolls' house furniture is legendary, and it would be a great pity if she had to stop producing it.'

'Actually, I think she's finding it a bit

of a struggle because of the arthritis in her hands, but she's not going to give in easily.'

'And nor should she. Anyway, John says he hopes to reopen again on Tuesday.'

He pulled up outside Rose Cottage, leant over and kissed her on the cheek.

'Things'll work out, you'll see. It's been a good evening, hasn't it?'

Aunt Rose was sitting over a mug of hot chocolate, watching the tail end of a documentary.

'Hello, dear. I thought you'd be a lot later than this. Did you enjoy your evening?'

'Yes, it was a lovely meal. How about you?'

Aunt Rose beamed, 'I had a lovely time too. They made me so welcome. Fiona's mum, Betty, is a widow and she's decided to sell up and move down here as soon as it can be arranged. We got on really well.'

'That's good.' Sophie hesitated. She didn't like to mention Peggy Munn's shop being closed, but knew she'd better fill Aunt Rose in so that she didn't hear the news in church the following morning.

'Well, I can't say I'm surprised, but it's a dreadful shame. I wonder if I could fit in any more hours down there, although I'm not too keen to do it on my own!'

'I could probably manage another session. We'll have to get our heads together,' Sophie told her. 'By the way, I was interested to learn that Keir is still in contact with Erica. Beverley asked him outright.'

'Well, I suppose if he's renting her house then he's got to be. I don't see anything strange in that, Sophie. I just hope that if she does decide to sell Rowanbank, she gives Keir first refusal.'

So did Sophie. Suddenly the thought of being in Penbridge without Keir seemed something she really didn't want to contemplate. He had given her a new purpose in life, melted the ice around her heart and made her come alive again.

Work was a great deal easier the following week apart from Stanley Pierce who made it clear that he'd rather Sophie wasn't there.

'All the other support staff have worked outside in a separate area. It's less distracting,' he told her.

When she arrived back at Rose Cottage she found Aunt Rose sitting at the kitchen table, eyes glistening with tears.

'Whatever's wrong?' Sophie asked, alarmed.

'It's Peggy. John's just called in to give me the key on his way to work, and he's told me the news.'

'Is she worse?' Sophie prompted, sitting opposite Aunt Rose.

'No, no, it's not that. She's on the mend. But she's finally thrown in the towel and decided to move nearer to them, which will mean giving up the shop. John says he'll endeavour to keep it open for about three afternoons a week, just until the property is sold. Actually, he's offered to pay me to do a bit more sorting out. Apparently, Peggy's perfectly happy for me to do that and there's a cupboard jam-packed with stock. He'll have a clearance sale eventually. It's a bit of a body blow, Sophie, I have to tell you.'

'I'm so sorry, Aunt Rose. I can't imagine how you must be feeling,' Sophie said sympathetically.

Aunt Rose blew her nose and got briskly to her feet. 'Well, I'd better not sit here all day. There's work to be done. Have you had any lunch, Sophie?'

'Not yet, but I can grab something from the baker's once we've opened up.' She picked up the box of dolls' house furniture from the table and they set off.

They spent the afternoon sorting through previously unopened boxes and labelling them ready for John to see, only stopping to serve the occasional customer.

'I knew Peggy was a hoarder, but this is ridiculous,' Rose said mopping her brow.

'We ought to get Keir to take a look. He'd know if there was anything of value and then, with John and Peggy's permission, we could organise some kind of sale.'

It seemed that no sooner had the words left Sophie's mouth than Keir appeared.

'I've just popped in to see how things are going and to find out if you want a lift to the class tonight. My goodness, whatever's all this?'

'About five years' worth of new stock, I would imagine. It's such a mixture that we're going to have a problem pricing it up.'

Keir consulted his watch. 'I could spare half-an-hour or so, if that would help, just to separate the more expensive items from the junk.'

'Oh, I don't like doing this without Peggy's say so. It doesn't seem right somehow,' Aunt Rose said worriedly.

'Well, we're not actually proposing to sell anything not already on display without consulting either Peggy or John, are we now?' Sophie pointed out.

Keir made a quick assessment of the stuff they had unearthed so far. They found a marker and some labels and repacked the boxes once they'd been sorted.

'How many more of these boxes are there?'

For an answer Rose led him to the back of the shop and flung back an ancient velvet curtain to reveal a series of shelves from floor to ceiling, stacked high with cardboard boxes of all shapes and sizes.

'Quite an eye opener, isn't it? No wonder John and his wife haven't a clue where to begin.'

'Mind if I take a look?' Keir asked.

'Feel free.'

Rose went off to serve a customer and Sophie lingered as Keir cast his eyes over the boxes. 'Most of these look like new stock. Even I would need a ladder to reach that top shelf.'

Sophie fetched the stepstool and he hoisted himself up.

He spent several minutes looking at the labels on the boxes, pausing over one or two. When he clambered down again he dusted down his trousers and she noted the thoughtful expression on his face.

'Keir, what is it? What exactly have you discovered up there?'

'I'm not sure — something or nothing. Leave it with me for the moment. Sophie, you're not working tomorrow afternoon, are you?'

'No, why?'

'Neither am I. Could you spare the time to come back here for an hour or two, with the Munns' permission, of course.'

Rose finished dealing with the customer and joined them at the back of the shop.

'Have you found some buried treasure, Keir?'

'I doubt it, but there is a bit of a

puzzle and I'd like to come back tomorrow when I've got a bit more time. I'm afraid I'll have to go now or I won't be ready for my class this evening and that would never do, would it, Sophie?'

'Well, what do you make of that?' Rose asked as the door closed behind him.

'I can't make out what he could have seen just by looking at the outside of some boxes,' Sophie added, staring up at the shelves as if seeking inspiration.

'We're just going to have to be patient, aren't we?'

Back at Rowanbank, Keir picked up the phone to Erica. To his surprise, she answered almost as soon as it started ringing. After exchanging a few pleasantries, he came to the point.

'Erica have you had occasion to take any boxes of ornaments to Peggy Munn's shop?'

'What are you talking about, Keir? Why would I? Oh, wait a minute, I remember now, but that was yonks ago, when I was clearing out a cupboard in the spare room. I'd forgotten all about it. Why?'

'Because . . . ' He filled her in and asked a few pertinent questions.

'As if I would! Honestly, Keir, if you're right then it was a genuine mistake. You know what Hugh was like about getting rid of things. I just had to get on and do it myself. How was I to know? It just looked like a load of old junk to me — otherwise, why would it have been stowed in that cupboard? Anyway, you were left all the ceramics so, by rights, I suppose all that stuff's yours. What's that? Keir, if you haven't even looked inside the boxes then why on earth are you making such a fuss?'

She listened impatiently for a few moments. 'No, of course not. What? OK, I'll leave it in your capable hands. I'm sure you can sort it out. If not I'll get in touch with the people concerned. What a bore! Anyway, it could just be a load of old junk. Now we've got friends coming over tonight, so I'll have to love you and leave you. Bye for now.'

Keir sighed as he put down the phone. Erica really was the limit. If his suspicions were right then it was a mercy Peggy Munn was such a hoarder. He consulted his watch and went into the study.

# 'Someone Hurt You Badly'

'I've managed to get hold of John Munn,' Keir told Sophie on the way to the class that evening. 'He's perfectly happy for me to take a look at the contents of the boxes and make a list. Apparently his mother just doesn't feel up to doing it herself and has agreed to him taking charge, but obviously he'll have to run everything past her before disposing of any of the stock.'

'I take it there's something that's gripped your attention,' Sophie prompted.

'I'd rather not say for the moment. After all, it could be that the boxes have been recycled, in which case I'd have egg on my face if I told you what I was thinking.'

'Right then, I'll just have to wait until tomorrow afternoon, won't I?'

'Yes, I'm afraid we both will,' he said, as he drove through the school gateway.

Keir had already unloaded the kiln and everyone crowded round to take a look at their efforts. 'Today comes the exciting bit,' Keir told them. 'We'll be decorating the jewellery prior to refiling it and then, next week, we can adhere clips and fastenings.'

Keir took the cufflinks he had been working on and showed them carefully how to apply metallic lustre bands to their jewellery. 'It will just add the finishing touch.'

After this, they began to make dishes using moulds. It was during the break that one of the students asked, 'Have we had any sales yet from Mrs Munn's shop?'

'I wouldn't hold your breath?' Glenda said rudely.

'You'll be pleasantly surprised,' Keir told them. 'Yes, there have been several sales, but I'm afraid you'll have to wait a while for your payment, as the lady who runs the shop is indisposed and her son is dealing with it. I have it on the best authority, however, that we can continue to use the shop as an outlet for our wares. It'll continue to open three or four times a week.'

'That seems very positive,' Crystal remarked. 'Poor Mrs Munn has been very poorly with a nasty cold recently, which is why the shop's been closed more often.'

Sophie thought Glenda looked distinctly uncomfortable, but she didn't make any further comment.

The evening passed pleasantly enough and Sophie realised that, although she enjoyed what she was doing, she was just happy to be in Keir's company.

When they'd finished clearing up the room, someone suggested they went for a drink. One or two of the group had to get home, but several of them, including Glenda, Crystal and Alan opted to go to the nearby pub. It was a relaxing atmosphere and Sophie watched Keir as he interacted with the other members of the group. He was such a charming, considerate man and she knew she was in danger of falling in love with him.

Was she deluding herself when she felt he was interested in her? After all, apart from that one kiss there had been nothing to indicate that he thought of her as anyone special.

Glenda said something in a low voice and he roared with laughter. Sophie couldn't help but feel a tinge of jealousy.

After one drink the group split up, most of them having work the following day.

'So we'll take a good look at those boxes tomorrow, shall we?' Keir asked Sophie on the way home.

'What about Peggy Munn? I wonder if she'll mind us going through her stock.'

'Oh, John will clear it — don't worry on that score,' he assured her. 'I get the impression that it's all been getting a bit much for her for rather a long time now and that, now that she's finally decided to retire, she doesn't want to be bothered with it any longer.'

'Well, that's as maybe,' Sophie said, 'but I still think we need to tread carefully. After all, it's been her livelihood for years now.'

'Oh, I'll see that she gets a good price for everything, if that's what's worrying you, Sophie.'

'No, I didn't mean . . . Keir, surely you didn't think . . . '

'I think you've got a highly suspicious mind,' he told her frankly. 'You have to learn to put your trust in people a bit more.'

It was a good job that it was dark because Sophie felt the colour flood her cheeks. He was right. The episode with Brett had left her unsure of herself and wary of trusting people.

When they pulled up outside Rose Cottage, Keir reached across and took her hands between his. 'Someone hurt you badly, didn't he? Perhaps one day you'll feel able to talk about it, but until then, remember that not everyone is like that.'

She lay awake for a long time that

night. Was she really so transparent that Keir was able to see into her heart? He was ten times the man Brett was. In that moment, she made up her mind to let go of the past and concentrate on the future.

\* \* \*

You'll never believe what I've done,' Aunt Rose greeted Sophie at breakfast the following morning. 'I've only double-booked myself. Should have looked on the calendar. I'm supposed to be at the vicarage this afternoon discussing church matters with the friends of St. Bartholomew's.'

'Right, that's no problem,' Sophie told her. 'Keir and I can manage perfectly well between us at the shop.'

'Well, if you're sure.' Aunt Rose hesitated. 'But what about locking up and setting the alarm? I don't think Peggy would be too happy if I gave the code out to all and sundry.'

Sophie laughed at this and Aunt Rose

clapped her hand to her mouth, as she realised what she'd said. 'Oh, you know what I meant, dear.'

'Yes, I'm only teasing. Don't worry about a thing. I'll sort it out with Keir,' and she picked up her mobile.

It was arranged that Sophie would drive Aunt Rose to the shop before John Munn left and that as soon as Keir arrived, Sophie would then transport Aunt Rose to the vicarage for her meeting. After Rose's meeting, Sophie would collect her, so that she could lock the shop and set the alarm.

'What a palaver!' Rose said. 'I'm getting forgetful in my old age!'

'Nonsense,' Keir said. 'You're just a spring chicken!' Rose dissolved into laughter and Sophie reflected that he was good with old and young alike.

★ ★ ★

'Right,' Keir said, once they were on their own in the gift shop. 'I've redone the window display whilst you were taking Rose to the vicarage. Shall we have a look at some of those boxes? I reckon there must be around thirty.'

Sophie whistled. 'As many as that! Where do we begin?'

'If you're in agreement, I'd actually like to start with the top shelf. There's something that's caught my attention.'

'I've gathered that, but you're obviously not prepared to tell me what it is, are you?'

'Patience is a virtue,' he said. 'Give me a hand, will you?' He clambered up the stepstool and perched precariously, stretching up to reach the top box which he then handed down to Sophie who placed it on the table. He brought down two more and said, 'That'll do for now. Shall we take a look?'

Sophie nodded. The boxes were sealed carefully with parcel tape and labelled in a bold marker, but then she gasped as she saw another label on the side which she recognised as being in Hugh's handwriting.

'These have come from Rowanbank, haven't they?'

He nodded. 'I don't want to say any more until I've had a chance to look at the contents.' He reached in the backpack he'd brought with him and produced a knife which he used to slit the tape. The first box revealed a number of objects wrapped in newspaper.

'We need a system, otherwise we'll have nowhere to put these and they'll ultimately have to be repackaged,' he told her.

Sophie found a wastepaper basket, scissors and sellotape and Keir impatiently cleared a space by putting a number of the display items on the floor. He then turned his attention to the contents of the box. Sophie watched in amazement as he unwrapped a number of pottery bowls and vases, some glass dishes and some wooden ornaments.

'I don't understand,' she said. 'What are all these things doing here?'

But Keir was studying the items, turning them this way and that, a preoccupied expression on his face.

'Right, there's not much to get excited about in that lot, so if we relabel the box we can eventually dispose of it. To answer your question, Sophie, I think someone was having a bit of a clearout and got over enthusiastic.'

The second box was much the same as the first — mainly bric-a-brac.

'Third time lucky,' Keir murmured, and shook his head as he unwrapped some of the stuff on the top of it. After a moment or two he looked up.

'It looks as if I might have been wrong, after all. What a disappointment!'

'Keir, I wish you'd tell me what it is you're looking for . . . '

'To be honest, I'm not sure, but when and if I come across it, I'll let you know.'

Several times they were interrupted by customers coming into the shop, plus one or two other folk who'd seen the shop open and wanted to enquire after Peggy Munn.

After they'd repacked and relabelled the third box Keir shimmied up the step stool yet again. Sophie watched as he reached up and exclaimed.

'There's one more here! I'd almost overlooked it! Fingers crossed, Sophie!'

'But I don't know what I'm crossing them for,' she protested laughingly and, stretching up, took the box from him.

First he unwrapped a couple of attractive pottery bowls.

'Ah, these are more like it. Now, what have we here?'

He moved aside a layer of newspaper and handed her a carefully wrapped parcel.

'This, I believe, is the property of your father.'

Sophie stared at Keir in astonishment. 'But how — what? I don't understand.'

He did not reply, being intent on rummaging further into the box before straightening up clasping another

241

smaller package. 'At last, I think this could well be Rose's inheritance. Wait a minute, there are more.'

Sophie looked at the carefully wrapped parcels and read the labels in Uncle Hugh's unmistakable writing.

'A voice from the grave,' she murmured. 'Did he give them to Peggy for safe-keeping and then she forgot about them?'

Keir shook his head. 'No, I think they were mistakenly brought here by Erica. I spoke to her on the phone last night.'

'Oh, I might have guessed Erica would have had a hand in it!'

His eyes blazed. 'And why aren't I surprised at your reaction?'

The pair of them stood glaring at each other for a moment and then Sophie said unsteadily, 'Why do you always stick up for her? What is it between the two of you?'

Keir paused for so long that she thought he wasn't going to reply and then he said in a low voice, 'Erica and I — we've been through a lot together. It will probably surprise you to know that she was with me at a charity dinner when I introduced her to Hugh.'

The knowledge sank in slowly. 'Right, but the fact remains that Erica denied all knowledge of the gifts Uncle Hugh had left Rose and my parents, but she obviously brought them here at some stage.'

'It was a mistake, Sophie. Don't judge her so harshly. She had no idea the packages were in those boxes. She wouldn't have done that intentionally. Anyway, the wretched things have been found now, so does it really matter how they came to be here?'

Sophie shook her head, not trusting herself to speak. There were so many unanswered questions.

Keir sighed. 'The problem is, we're going to have to clear this with Peggy Munn. Erica says she didn't receive any money for the boxes, because she agreed to wait until Peggy had sold the contents. Erica assures me she'd completely forgotten about them until I spoke to her, but technically, as they're on Peggy's property, I suppose we can't just walk off with them and so, for the time being, we'd better not raise your family's hopes by mentioning our find.'

'If you say so.'

Keir saw the crestfallen expression on her face and, moving towards her, caught her hands in his. 'I know how much this means to you.'

'I just wanted to sort it out. Uncle Hugh intended Aunt Rose and my parents to have a keepsake that he had selected for them. Aunt Rose loves the bowl you gave her for her birthday, but although it belonged to Hugh and Mary, it isn't quite the same as if they had intended it for her, is it?'

His expression softened. 'You're a very caring person, Sophie,' he said gently. 'We'll sort it out.'

Keir turned back to the box. 'I thought I'd completely emptied this, but there's something else.'

He removed another package and unwrapped it carefully to reveal an exquisite pair of ceramic candlesticks.

'I don't believe it — no wonder Erica said she couldn't find these!'

He set them down on the counter and then picking one up, turned it over in his hand.

'Hugh bought them for Erica for their first wedding anniversary,' he said slowly. 'I thought she would treasure them.'

'Perhaps she didn't realise they were in the box with the other things.'

'Thanks, Sophie. I'd truly like to think that was the case,' he said gruffly.

'Were they made by the same potter as the other pieces Hugh left you?' she asked quietly.

He nodded, as if not trusting himself to speak and bowed his head, but not before she had seen the raw emotion in his eyes. She moved to his side and caught his arm.

'Tell me, Keir. What happened.'

He shook his head and suddenly she was in his arms and he was kissing her, but the kisses were bittersweet because she sensed he was still swamped by memories of the past.

'Tell me, Keir,' she said again, when they drew apart.

For an answer he placed a finger on her lips.

'I will, I promise — very soon, and you must tell me your story too.'

She was saved from replying because the shop door jangled just then and Aunt Rose came in carrying another box of eggs.

'Frances gave me a lift on her way to collect the children from school.' She looked from one to the other. 'Is everything all right?'

'Yes, indeed,' Keir replied. 'Very all right. We've had an extremely productive afternoon. We've sorted through some of those boxes, and it only remains for me to speak to John Munn before we can dispose of the contents.'

Sophie caught his gaze and realised that she'd need to keep very quiet about their find for the time being.

There was something else she was

going to have to keep to herself too — the knowledge that she was in love with Keir Ellison.

Once he had seen the contents of the boxes from Rowanbank, John Munn did not waste any time. Keir phoned Sophie to tell her that John had spoken with his mother, who vaguely remembered Erica bringing the boxes to the shop. Who had been responsible for stacking them on the top shelf was a mystery in itself.

Peggy said that it was highly unlikely that she would have paid Erica anything until there had been a sale, but there ought to be some sort of record in her stock books.

John promised he'd take a look and get back to them as soon as possible and that in the meantime, Peggy insisted that the parcels that were very clearly labelled, should be handed to the people they were intended for.

Keir thought the right thing to do would be to contact the solicitor on Monday. In the meantime, they agreed to remain silent on the issue.

After they'd finished discussing this over the phone, Keir said casually, 'Sophie, I realise this is very short notice, but I thought I'd have a run down to Rye tomorrow. There's a pottery I'd like to take a look at so, if you're free, I was wondering if you'd care to come along?'

'That'd be great,' she assured him, her heart pounding. 'I haven't got anything planned apart from going to the farm shop for Aunt Rose.'

'Right, if you can fit that in early, I could pick you up by ten,' he said. 'Have you been to Rye before?'

'I'm not sure — maybe when I was a child. It's in Sussex, isn't it?'

'Certainly is. Medieval flavour, cobbled streets, harbour, one of the Cinque Ports — ring any bells?'

'Probably, in the dim and distant past.'

★　★　★

The weekend which had previously seemed as if it would be uneventful, now took on a new dimension. Sophie knew that every moment spent with Keir would be precious. She told herself she mustn't read too much into his kisses which she accepted had been something to do with the candlesticks — something that she didn't understand.

She supposed Keir would confide in her in his own good time, but for now she was determined just to enjoy his company.

They set off soon after ten o'clock. It was a bright February morning and here and there they spotted clumps of snowdrops and bright yellow splashes of aconites in people's gardens. They could see for miles across a rather stark landscape which Sophie knew would come alive as spring approached.

There was so much to see and do in Rye that they were spoilt for choice. First they visited the pottery where Keir spent a long time examining the goods in the showroom.

Sophie was fascinated by the exquisite, Majolica figures of animals and birds and wondered if she'd ever aspire to making such things herself.

When they eventually moved away Keir said, 'Let's have some lunch. I'm absolutely ravenous!'

Over a fish lunch in a charming restaurant, housed in a building dating from the 1800s Keir said, 'I really enjoy your company, Sophie and I'd like to get to know you better.'

'So, what do you want to know?' she asked tentatively.

'Everything. I really want to find out what makes you tick. Tell me about the times you spent in Penbridge when you stayed at Rowanbank.'

They exchanged anecdotes about university days and holidays and she discovered Keir had a married sister and a mother living in Gloucestershire. By the time they'd finished coffee she realised they'd both skated round anything to do with past relationships.

'So how did you come to meet Uncle Hugh?' she asked casually.

'Oh, at a pottery exhibition up in London. We got talking and after that we kept in touch.'

She hazarded a guess. 'Would I be right in thinking it was an exhibition of that potter's work you both admired so much?'

She could tell from the expression on his face that she was right.

'Was that pure conjecture or did someone . . . ?'

Sophie shook her head. 'I realise she obviously meant a lot to the pair of you. I saw the way you reacted over those candlesticks — remember?'

He nodded and his brown eyes clouded. 'I still find it difficult to talk about — the same as I'm aware there are things you'd prefer not to mention, such as your reason for leaving the school where Peter Standish used to be deputy head.'

She lowered her gaze. 'OK, I expect we all have our Achille's heel.'

'They say time is a great healer so let's hope they're right,' he said softly.

Afterwards they sauntered hand in hand along Mermaid Street, a cobbled lane full of medieval buildings. They stopped to admire the famous Mermaid Inn.

'I was reading that in the eighteenth century, this place used to be the headquarters of a famous band of smugglers called the Hawkhurst Gang,' Keir informed her. 'Now, what would you like to do next? It's a bit cold to hang about, but we could take a look at the antique glass shop, just as a change from ceramics.'

'Brilliant idea!' she told him, as they wandered round the most amazing display of glassware she had ever seen in her life.

'Once the craft centre is up and running, we're going to need to keep our options open. Several of the units are allocated already and we're only interested in fairly high class stuff. We hope to have an area to encourage talented youngsters to work and exhibit their creations.'

'Was that Uncle Hugh's idea too?' she asked.

'Yes, he was so enthusiastic. It's one of the reasons I came to Penbridge.'

Sophie wondered what the others were. There was so much about Keir she still needed to discover. 'Penbridge is a lovely spot. Ever since I visited as a child, I've really loved it.'

'I suppose you knew Rowanbank pretty well — all its nooks and crannies?'

She smiled, remembering her childhood.

'Oh, yes, my brother, myself and Crystal Briggs used to play hide and seek, but Crystal's older sister — Amy's mum — thought she was too old to play with us.'

'You'll have to show me some photos sometime. I bet you were a cute little girl.'

'I don't know about that. Actually, I was a bit of an untidy tomboy, always climbing trees.'

He chuckled.

The light was fading as they began their homeward journey and she didn't want the day to end. He said, 'How about us rounding off the day over dinner?'

Her heart pounded. 'I'd love to do that, Keir. The only problem is, I'm not the slightest bit hungry.'

He laughed. 'Well, I am. I could eat for England! Tell you what, how about coming back to Rowanbank and we can have omelettes and salad. You can always phone Rose so that she knows you'll be a bit late.'

'Oh, she won't mind. She's going to see a film in the village hall with some friends from church — except I did arrange to run her down there for seven o'clock.'

'Were you intending to join them?' he asked.

'Only if I hadn't been doing anything else. Actually, I've seen the film before so I wasn't that bothered.'

'I'm flattered you've chosen me over

a film,' he teased. 'Now, you transport Rose whilst I prepare a salad, by which time you might have worked up an appetite.'

It was almost eight o'clock by the time Sophie arrived at Rowanbank. She'd considered changing into something more dressy, but decided against it. She freshened up and put on a pretty jumper, and redid her hair and make-up.

Keir came to the door with a tea-towel over his arm. 'Madame, if I may take your coat, your table awaits.'

Sophie laughed and allowed him to help her off with her coat, catching her breath as she felt his body close to hers.

'I've just got the omelettes to make. There's ham, cheese and mushroom for fillings.'

'Sounds wonderful.'

Keir ushered her into the dining room where the table was already set with an immaculate white cloth, gleaming cutlery and a candelabra. There was a wedding photograph of Hugh and

Erica on the unit.

Sophie had to admit that they looked blissfully happy and was surprised that Erica hadn't taken the photograph with her. In the glass section of the unit were the pieces of pottery Keir had displayed at the exhibition in the village hall. She wondered again about the potter. She had obviously been a close friend of his — a girlfriend perhaps?

A few minutes later, they were tucking into fluffy omelettes and winter salad, washed down with glasses of white wine.

He had turned on the wall lights and soft music played from the expensive music centre. It was a romantic atmosphere and she felt totally relaxed in his company, loving every minute of it.

This time they talked about their childhood and schooldays. They ate one of Mrs Briggs cherry pies for dessert with ice cream, and then they moved into the sitting room and sat over coffee.

Keir joined Sophie on the sofa and it seemed natural when his arm slid round her waist. Suddenly, she was in his arms and he was stroking her hair and kissing her.

'Thank you for a delightful day, Sophie. I enjoy being with you so much. We haven't known each other very long, but there's an undeniable bond between us.'

She leant against him, feeling the warmth emanating from his muscular body, and this time when his lips met hers it was beyond her wildest dreams. His kisses set her on fire.

She drifted away on a cloud of euphoria, nestling against him. The sound of the front door closing shot them apart.

'What on earth?' Keir sprang to his feet.

'Burglars don't usually use the front entrance. Could it be Mrs Briggs?'

Keir's tensed. Just as he reached the door it opened. The woman who stood there looked as if she'd stepped off the front of a fashion magazine.

Keir was the first to speak. 'Erica! I hadn't expected to see you!'

'Obviously not! Don't I deserve a kiss, darling?'

Keir obliged.

Sophie stood, as if rooted to the spot. After a moment or two, during which Erica Mercer shrugged off her fur-trimmed coat and slung it over a chair, Keir propelled Sophie forward, his hand on her elbow.

'Erica, this is Hugh's cousin's daughter, Sophie Burnett.'

'Oh, yes, I thought I'd seen you somewhere before.'

For a moment it was as if Sophie had been struck dumb, but then she felt Keir behind her, his hand gently resting on her arm.

'I'm staying with Rose Harding,' she said, when she finally managed to find her voice.

Erica's green eyes glinted. 'Right — that's one of the reasons I'm here — to sort out all this wretched business over the stuff Hugh's supposed to have left Rose and your father. So tiresome to have all this hassle, although it's given me an opportunity to see Keir.'

Sophie felt slightly faint. 'It's time I was going,' she said, forcing herself to sound normal.

'Yes, if you don't mind,' Erica said dismissively. 'Keir and I have rather a lot to discuss, haven't we, darling?' She moved to a side table and poured herself a glass of wine and, as she did so, Sophie noticed the engagement ring.

It was not the one Hugh had given Erica, which had been sapphire and diamonds in an antique setting. No, this was a modern design — an ostentatious cluster of diamonds.

Sophie felt her throat constricting, mesmerised by the sight of the ring. She could not bear to look at Keir. He didn't say anything merely nodded in reply to Erica who caught his arm.

Sophie could not escape from the room quickly enough. It was less than a year since Hugh had died and Erica was engaged again.

Sophie swallowed. She and Keir had been having such a wonderful day. Now she didn't know what to think. Surely, he and Erica . . . ? She shook her head, as if to rid herself of the thought.

They were obviously more than just friends. Keir hadn't attempted to persuade Sophie to stay and Erica had kissed him warmly.

Had he been leading Sophie on, just amusing himself until Erica's return? The tears blurred her eyes and she dashed them away angrily.

★ ★ ★

The following morning over breakfast, Aunt Rose stared at Sophie in disbelief.

'You're telling me Erica's returned and she's wearing an engagement ring?'

Sophie patted Aunt Rose's arm sympathetically. 'I'm so sorry, but I had to tell you before someone else did, and I didn't want to spoil your evening out.'

Aunt Rose nodded. 'Thank you for that, dear. It was a very good film. Well, I've no idea what to make of all this. I suppose Erica's met someone in Spain.'

If only that were the case. Sophie couldn't trust herself to voice her thoughts. She'd tossed and turned most of the night, trying to make sense of it all. She felt a deep pain inside her, as the realisation dawned that Keir was no better than Brett when it came to deceit.

* * *

Back at Rowanbank, Keir was finding it hard to have his space suddenly invaded by Erica. She had swept in like a whirlwind, full of demands, and didn't seem to realise the mayhem she was causing.

He'd seen the hurt in Sophie's eyes, the unspoken questions.

If only Erica's arrival could have been timed a bit differently. If only she hadn't barged in like that. There was so much he needed to say to Sophie and now he'd have to postpone it. He had thought their relationship was going places, but now, thanks to Erica, it was in danger of falling apart.

'I could have wished you'd have given me a little warning, Erica, rather than turning up out of the blue like this,' he said, as they sat over a late breakfast.

Erica buttered a croissant. 'Oh, you know me, darling. I do things on an impulse, but I would remind you that Rowanbank is still my house, so surely I can come and go as I please.' She put a hand on his sleeve. 'Anyway, you're full of surprises yourself, aren't you, darling? I wouldn't have thought that mousy little creature was your type, Keir.'

'Then that just shows how little you know about me, doesn't it?' he said curtly. 'Now, if you'll excuse me, I've got rather a lot of school work to do this morning.'

'So, what am I supposed to do whilst

you're doing that?' Erica demanded petulantly.

'I don't know — paint your nails, read the newspaper, find something in the freezer for lunch,' he said testily.

'Oh, you can take me out for lunch,' she told him airily. 'You know how I detest cooking. What about these wretched boxes. Can't I take a look at those to stop me dying from boredom?'

Keir frowned. 'You know you can't, Erica. We've discussed that already. That's mainly why you're here, isn't it, so that you can sort the matter out with John Munn and his mother. You'll need to contact your solicitor first thing tomorrow. I'm working, but if you want me to come with you, I could probably . . . '

'That's sweet of you, Keir, but unless you don't trust me to sort it out, I'll manage perfectly well on my own,' she told him firmly.

He didn't bother to reply, merely cleared his breakfast dishes and went into the study, closing the door behind him.

Erica reached for her mobile, a slight smile playing about her lips. The sooner she could get all this business over and done with the sooner she could get on with the real purpose of her visit.

# A Painful Return

Crystal was bursting to tell Sophie something when they met up after church.

'You'll never believe what I've just heard.'

'If it's to do with Erica Mercer then yes, I would. How did you know? There seems to be a bush telegraph in this village.'

Crystal looked disappointed. 'Keir rang Mum just before we left for church. I suppose we shouldn't be too surprised. After all Rowanbank is still Erica's property. Anyway, it seems neither of them are likely to be around when Mum does the cleaning tomorrow morning.'

'OK, well, here's something you won't know. Erica is wearing a large diamond engagement ring,' Sophie told her friend and waited for her reaction.

Crystal was suitably surprised. 'You're kidding me! Well, she doesn't believe in letting the grass grow, does she? Any idea who the guy is?'

She saw the expression on Sophie's face and her eyes widened. 'Oh, Sophie, surely not! You must have got it wrong . . . ' She trailed off as her mother and Rose caught up with them.

★ ★ ★

That afternoon, Sophie threw herself wholeheartedly into helping Aunt Rose with the dolls' house furniture. Later, after they had enjoyed a cosy tea in the sitting room, she indulged Aunt Rose by looking through some old photograph albums.

'My goodness you and Aunt Mary were almost identical!'

'In looks maybe, but our personalities were very different. I was born first. Mary was slightly smaller and always the weaker one. For that reason she always seemed to get her own way.'

Sophie looked at Aunt Rose in surprise. She'd always thought the sisters had been very close, but now she detected the slightest trace of bitterness in Aunt Rose's voice. 'When Mary married Hugh, our parents were still renting Laburnum Cottage from Hugh's parents. These two cottages were part of the estate. It was an awkward situation, as you can imagine, so the rent was waived and then, when Hugh's parents died, he inherited the whole estate and gifted both cottages to Mary. Eventually, when our own parents had also passed away, she chose to sell our old home, but to keep this one.'

Sophie tried to get her head round this. 'So are you saying you still pay rent to Erica?'

'Oh, no, dear. Mary left Rose Cottage to Tom and I . . . ' She trailed off, as a thought suddenly occurred to her. 'You don't suppose that's what Hugh meant, do you? Something of value that you've already got.'

Sophie's eyes widened. 'Well, I

suppose he might have done, except it wasn't Hugh who gave you this cottage, was it? It was Mary and, if you look at it a different way, you and Uncle Tom, and his family before him, had been paying rent to Hugh's family for it.'

Aunt Rose's face cleared. 'Yes, you're right, dear. Well, it's no good thinking about it. We're not likely to solve the mystery, so we might as well forget about it.'

Sophie kept very quiet, determined not to say anything about the boxes they'd found.

*　*　*

Sophie dreaded bumping into Keir, afraid that she might give her feelings away. She couldn't avoid him at school, however, and found it difficult to concentrate during his pottery class.

A plaintive voice beside her wailed, 'I can't do it, Miss! This pot's rubbish!'

Sophie endeavoured to help the young lad in her charge, but was all fingers and thumbs.

Seeing her predicament, Keir came across to sort it out. She was so aware of him as he leant across the table, and had a strong desire to reach out and touch him. Her emotions were in turmoil. At the end of the lesson, after the students had gone, Keir said, 'We need to talk, Sophie.'

'Do we?' she asked shakily, gathering her possessions together.

'You know we do! I don't know what ideas you've got in your head, but we need to sort things out between us. Quite apart from which, there's good news concerning those gifts intended for Rose and your parents. Erica went to her solicitor on Monday and Mr Hodge has arranged to come to Rowanbank on Friday and to distribute the items from there. Would you like to inform Rose or shall I? Obviously James Hodge will be getting in touch with both her and your parents.'

'Right,' Sophie said. 'I'll leave it to you then, as you've been dealing with it.

Now, if you'll excuse me, I must grab a quick lunch.'

She couldn't meet his eyes, afraid of what she might read in them. As she opened the door, his hand shot out and caught her wrist, and it felt as if his fingers were burning into her flesh.

'If you'd just let me explain about Erica and me . . . ' he began.

'There's no need — absolutely none of my concern,' she told him, shaking off his hand impatiently and turning, walked swiftly away down the corridor leaving him staring after her, wishing he'd been more upfront with her from the beginning.

He couldn't bear to lose her, but until she'd arrived at Rose Cottage he'd truly believed there would never be another woman in his life after Nina. He sighed and asked himself for the umpteenth time why on earth Erica had had to complicate matters by her untimely and unannounced arrival. Although, he still wasn't quite sure why Sophie was so angry with him.

# A Time for Truth

On his way home, Keir dropped into Rose Cottage to see Rose. Sophie was at a meeting and Rose suspected he knew this. She took one look at his face and put the kettle on.

'I understand Erica's returned to Rowanbank,' she said, as she fetched the cups and saucers from the dresser. Keir examined the china thoughtfully.

'Yes, but she's up in London today. The thing is, Rose, we think we might have solved the problem of the missing gifts Hugh referred to in those letters left with the will. You see, Sophie and I were sorting through some of those boxes last week . . . '

'Go on . . . ' Rose made the tea, poured Keir a cup and pushed the biscuit tin towards him.

Keir wished Sophie was there, sitting beside him at the table and was at a loss as to know how to put matters right between them. He sipped his tea, took a deep breath and attempted to explain to Rose Harding about the packages they'd discovered in the boxes.

'Well, the pair of you have been busy,' Rose commented when he'd finished. 'And you say Erica's been to see her solicitor?'

'Yes, on Monday. At his request, John Munn's been to see him too — with the packages. Mr Hodge has stipulated that the items will either have to be collected from his office or he'll distribute them from Rowanbank on Friday. Apparently, he needs signatures.'

'Well, I know James Hodge — Friday you say? I'll get Sophie to speak to her parents tonight. Hopefully, they'll be able to come then. They were going to visit us soon anyway.'

Keir cleared his throat. 'Sophie and I — well, I'm afraid there's been a bit of a misunderstanding. You see, Erica turned up at a rather inopportune moment and I believe Sophie's got the wrong end of the stick.'

Rose Harding threw caution to the wind. 'Keir, I've never pried into your personal life before. You wouldn't have thanked me if I had, but perhaps you could just answer one question for me now, please?'

Keir turned a troubled gaze to Rose. 'What's that?'

'Are you engaged to Erica Mercer?'

He paused for so long that she thought he couldn't have heard the question. She was about to repeat it when he said, 'No, Rose, I am not engaged to Erica — whatever gave you that extraordinary idea?'

'I think you'll find it's what Sophie believes.'

Keir was astounded. 'But what on earth would make her think . . . '

'Well, for starters, apparently Erica's wearing a rather flashy engagement ring — to say nothing of the fact that you two seem very friendly,' Rose said quietly.

Keir's face was a picture. 'Right

— well I can assure you I'm not engaged to Erica or anyone else. Erica and I have known each other for a number of years. Circumstances have thrown us together.' Keir hesitated. 'Rose, I really need to tell Sophie this myself, and I've been waiting for the right moment. It's not the easiest of things for me to talk about, but . . . '

Rose sat and listened to Keir's story and, when he'd finished, she placed her hand over his. 'Oh, Keir. I'm so sorry. Life certainly deals some cruel blows, doesn't it? Who else knows?'

'My headmaster and his wife and a couple of my work colleagues. I was hoping that Sophie and I could exchange confidences. I felt we were forming a good relationship, but now she seems so distant.'

'You must talk to her, Keir,' Rose advised. 'The problem is that she had her confidence severely shaken by a previous relationship and so, if she thinks she can't trust you . . . '

He nodded. 'I'm aware of that. Do

you know what happened? Has she confided in you?'

'No. I only know what her parents have told me. How long is Erica proposing to stay at Rowanbank?'

'Oh, she's just here to tie up a few loose ends. Hugh's will was rather complicated.'

'And this man she's engaged to?'

'It's her news — I'll leave it to her to tell you,' Keir said. 'Now, about that other matter. Can I leave it to you to sort it out with Sophie's parents? James Hodge will be in touch before Friday. You're all invited to stay on to lunch at Rowanbank after the business side of things is concluded. Mrs Briggs has agreed to provide a cold buffet and I'm sure she'll do us proud.'

Rose Harding made a sudden decision. Much as it went against the grain for her to set foot in Rowanbank whilst it still belonged to Erica Mercer, she was curious to know what James Hodge had to say about the packages found at Peggy Munn's.

'Thank you, Keir, that would be very nice.'

Rose would go over to Rowanbank and would be civil and she just hoped that Erica Mercer would be the same.

# Words of Love

'I don't know what all the fuss is about,' Erica told Keir that evening. 'Why do we have to have these people over here, when James Hodge could perfectly well go to Rose Cottage?'

'Erica! I know there's no love lost between you and Rose and, to a degree, I can understand why things are awkward between the pair of you, but on this occasion, I really think it would be good if you could bury the hatchet and — well, be gracious. After all, although it wasn't deliberate, you did make rather a bad error when you left those boxes with Peggy Munn.'

Erica pouted. 'Oh, if you say so, darling. It's such a pity Carlos is still in Spain, but his business is important to him. Now the most important thing on my agenda is to put Rowanbank on the market as soon as possible.'

Keir stared at her in disbelief. 'You're not serious?'

Erica smoothed back her blonde hair. 'Deadly. We initially agreed that you'd stay here until Hugh's affairs were sorted out and the craft centre got off the ground.'

Keir rubbed his chin. 'Yes, but that was then. Now things are different. Erica, would you be prepared to wait just for another week or two?'

She considered. 'I'll speak to Carlos — see what he has to say. Anyway, I'm not likely to sell this place overnight, am I? You'd have plenty of time to scout around and find somewhere else, darling. To be honest, I can't wait to get rid of the place. I never did like this house and now there are far too many memories.'

Keir did not reply. He was staring at a photograph of Hugh and Erica, as if trying to make sense of everything.

★ ★ ★

Sophie's parents agreed to come to Penbridge on Friday.

'It's a bit short notice, but your father has some time owing to him and his boss is very understanding,' her mother told her over the phone. 'This is all very mysterious — and you say you were there when this neighbour of Rose's discovered the packages in Peggy Munn's shop?'

'That's right. Well, I'll look forward to your visit on Friday, although I don't suppose I'll see much of you as you're going over to Rowanbank almost as soon as you arrive. You'll have to get back early for Gran, won't you?'

'No, June's visiting her mother and your gran's been invited along too. She gets on well with Sylvia. Anyway, surely you'll be coming over to Rowanbank with us?'

'Hardly, none of this concerns me, does it? I don't think I'm invited.'

'Well, not for the business part maybe, but surely to lunch,' her mother said thoughtfully. 'Now, what do you know about this man Erica's engaged to?'

What could Sophie say about Keir? She realised that he'd become such a large part of her life so quickly. She found herself thinking about him every waking hour and she didn't want to go over to Rowanbank to see him with Erica. Sophie knew she was hopelessly in love with him herself.

★　★　★

'Could you do something for me, Sophie?' Aunt Rose asked the following evening.

'Well, of course, if I can.'

'Oh, it's nothing very arduous. I've forgotten to return this recipe book to Mavis Briggs and she can collect it tomorrow when she's at Rowanbank. Apparently, Erica's got her doing some extra jobs. So, if you can drop it over there for me and take some of these cheese scones I've made for Keir. I know he's partial to them.'

Sophie could hardly refuse without seeming churlish.

It was a chilly evening and Sophie stood on the step at Rowanbank ringing the bell and rehearsing in her mind what to say.

A few moments later, Keir opened the door and the words went completely out of her head.

'Hello, Sophie. Won't you come in?' he invited, giving her a warm smile.

When Sophie hesitated, Keir caught her by the arm and drew her inside before she could come up with a suitable excuse.

'It's far too cold to stand on the step,' he told her firmly.

She held out the book and the scones and explained briefly.

'I'm putting on pounds. All these ladies keep feeding me up — including the canteen staff at school. Come and have some coffee. It's OK, Erica's visiting friends, if that's what's bothering you. Come on Sophie, it's high time we had that talk.'

'I'm not sure there would be any point,' she said unsteadily.

'OK, we'll have to see about that, won't we?'

Reluctantly, she followed him into the sitting room.

'Coffee — or I could run to a glass of wine — but promise me you won't escape whilst I'm getting it.'

'Coffee will be fine.' She smiled, and sank back on the sofa, knowing she was incapable of moving, even if she wanted to. Her legs had turned to jelly. She supposed she could at least hear him out.

He returned in a short space of time with a tray of coffee and a plate of Aunt Rose's scones.

After a moment or two she said, 'So what exactly did you want to talk to me about?'

'First and foremost, Erica is not engaged to me,' he told her. 'I can't blame you for jumping to conclusions, because I haven't exactly been open with you.'

'You've been talking to Aunt Rose,' she said unsteadily.

'Perhaps it's just as well I have, Sophie. I don't want to lose you and I need to explain so that you will understand. Erica was my sister-in-law — technically still is, I suppose.'

Sophie stared at him as if transfixed. 'Your sister-in-law!' she repeated incredulously. 'So what does that mean exactly? Are you married, divorced — separated?'

He shook his head. 'None of those — Nina, my wife, sadly died almost two years ago. She had a lengthy and painful illness.'

'Oh, Keir, I'm so very sorry. I had no idea.' She saw the sadness etching his face and wanted to put her arms around him and comfort him. No wonder he'd found it so difficult to talk about it with her.

They sat in silence for a few moments and then he said practically in a whisper, 'A relatively short time ago, I couldn't have mentioned Nina's name. We had a wonderful marriage and were drawn together by our love of ceramics.'

'Was she the talented potter you spoke of who made all those beautiful things you brought to the exhibition?' she prompted gently.

He nodded. 'We met at art college and got married soon after we graduated. Besides teaching part-time, we ran courses, held exhibitions and had studio open days — that sort of thing. Nina was incredibly talented, as you can see from her work.'

He pointed towards the wall unit. 'She was beginning to make a name for herself when her illness was first diagnosed and she struggled on, in between bouts of treatment and operations, until she became too weak to continue. She had tremendous will power and determination. It's what kept her alive for so long.'

'Oh, Keir, you must have had a dreadful time.'

'Yes, but strangely, it was during that period that I produced some of my best work. When Nina could no longer create her own ceramics, she took pleasure in what I was accomplishing. She was very unselfish.'

'And she was Erica's sister?'

He nodded. 'Erica and Nina were as different as chalk and cheese. Erica is a far more restless individual. She loves to travel — used to worked for an airline at one time. That's how she came to meet the man she's going to marry. She's known him for many years and he's asked her to marry him before. Probably, if she hadn't met Hugh, she would have done so. When Nina died, I'm afraid I became a bit of a recluse and Erica and Hugh were both very supportive. They persuaded me to do something in Nina's memory.'

'The craft centre?' she asked, as things began slowly to click into place.

'Yes. Hugh had been to several of Nina's exhibitions and knew how keen she'd been to promote fresh talent. The craft centre was very much his brain-child. That's why when Erica asked me if I could come here to carry on where he'd left off, in helping to set it up, I agreed. She's good at delegating — sometimes too good, I have to admit. Anyway, it gave me a purpose in life again and I've loved being here in Penbridge. It's given me a release and allowed me to move on with my life.'

He paused and they both sat deep in thought for a few moments. At last he looked up. 'So now that I've told you my story, perhaps you feel able to tell me yours.'

She smiled wryly. 'Oh, mine is nothing compared to yours. I just became involved with the wrong person. I thought Brett truly cared for me — that we had a future together, but then he went back to his former girlfriend, leaving me feeling betrayed and utterly bereft. But, you know what? It's all behind me now. At the time, I thought the bottom had dropped out of my world, but when I put it in perspective, so many good things have come about because of it.'

Sophie looked at Keir and felt a surge

of tenderness. 'If it hadn't been for what happened with Brett and myself, I wouldn't have come to Penbridge in January and met you.'

'And you have no idea how glad I am that you did,' he said softly.

The next moment, Keir had moved to sit beside her. He slipped an arm about her and drew her close. Cupping her chin in his hand, he kissed her mouth gently at first, but then, as she began to respond, more pasionately, until she was filled with a maelstrom of emotions. And this time Erica did not interrupt them.

As Sophie leant her head on his shoulder, Keir said, 'I didn't think I'd ever find love again after Nina. It was as if my heart was frozen, but you've changed all that. I don't want to lose you, Sophie, because I've fallen deeply in love with you.'

Reaching up she kissed him again. 'I love you too, Keir,' she murmured.

# A Truce is Called

Friday was a strange day, Sophie thought, as she joined her family in the sitting room at Rowanbank.

First Aunt Rose had been summoned to the study by James Hodge, who believed in doing things properly. She returned clutching two bulky packages and looking bemused.

It was the turn of David and Anne Burnett next, and they also reappeared with some packages which they placed alongside Rose's on the table.

Erica was then called into the study with Keir and John Munn.

Whilst they were gone Rose said, 'Well, I don't know about you two, but I'm itching to find out what Hugh has left me. James Hodge thinks these were probably intended to be given to us whilst Hugh was still alive, perhaps for a birthday or Christmas present, but he died before he got the chance.'

They watched with bated breath as she carefully unwrapped the first parcel to reveal a delicate antique vase. The other parcel contained the matching one to make up the pair.

Aunt Rose's eyes shone with pleasure. 'Hugh knew I'd always admired these. They used to stand on the mantelpiece in his study, and I quite thought Erica must have got rid of them. Well, of course, she nearly did! There's absolutely no way I'd ever sell them, even though James Hodge reckons they're probably quite valuable. Oh, my goodness, what's this?'

In her excitement, Aunt Rose had overlooked a small box which had been wedged between the two packages.

Removing the faded paper now, she revealed a jewellery case. Inside, on a bed of velvet, were two pairs of diamond earrings and an exquisite brooch.

Aunt Rose gasped and examined the earrings.

'These were Mary's. She had her ears

pierced and I didn't.'

'So they would be of no use to you unless you sold them,' David Burnett pointed out. 'They ought to bring you in quite a nice little nest egg.'

Aunt Rose's eyes were misty and she turned away for a moment.

'I knew Hugh wouldn't forget me,' she said huskily.

'Shall we see what we've got here?' Sophie's mother unwrapped one of the packages to reveal a beautiful Victorian watercolour which had previously hung on the sitting room wall.

In addition was a long box containing two Dresden china figurines. Yet another, smaller package contained a marquetry cigarette box concealing a pair of gold cuff links and a gold locket.

'My goodness! It's quite a treasure trove, isn't it!' Sophie exclaimed.

The others returned just then. John Munn looking very pleased about something, declined Keir's invitation to stay to lunch, saying that he'd have to return to work.

Lunch was a much more relaxed occasion now that most of the formalities were out of the way. Presently, they all proposed a toast to Hugh.

'Erica does have some more news,' Keir said turning to her.

Erica attempted a smile. 'Where to begin. Firstly, I had no idea Hugh had put all those valuable things in the boxes in the spare room. I assume he intended to distribute them as gifts, but his premature death prevented it.'

There was not much anyone could say to that, Sophie thought.

'Well, it's all been resolved now,' remarked Anne Burnett, always the peace maker.

'Practically, we're going to check out the rest of the boxes, sell anything Erica and I don't want and split the proceeds with Peggy Munn,' Keir informed them, which explained why John had looked so pleased.

James Hodge had kept very quiet

throughout all of this, but now he gave Erica a meaningful look.

She toyed with her wine glass for a moment before saying, 'I've come back here to wind things up. I'm going to be married again shortly and didn't want to leave unfinished business. Carlos and I have known each other for years, but I want you to know, Rose, that Hugh will always have a special place in my heart.'

Sophie realised it couldn't have been easy for Erica to have said that. This time, everyone raised their glasses to Erica.

James then leant towards Keir and murmured something. Keir nodded.

'There are still one or two other matters to discuss. Erica was intending to put Rowanbank on the market, but I've persuaded her not to, because I've decided I'd like to purchase it myself.'

Sophie's eyes locked with Keir's. This was the most wonderful news yet.

Keir smiled at her. 'I came to Penbridge feeling rather apprehensive. I wasn't sure how I'd fit into the community. You see, Erica had entrusted me to carry out a very special task for her. Sophie knows about most of this already and Rose knows a part of it . . .'

He faltered and Erica took over, explaining clearly and concisely about the craft centre project and how Hugh had been instrumental in getting it off the ground.

'It was his vision,' she said. 'Hugh was a very rich man and I can tell you now that he donated a considerable sum of money to the venture during his lifetime, and has left a sizeable bequest. But the rest is Keir's story . . .'

Keir picked up the story and this time managed to tell his audience briefly about Nina and how her work had won awards.

'I'm convinced that, given time, her work would have gained international acclaim.'

Keir went on to explain how Nina had worked from their home in Wiltshire and that, when she'd died, Hugh had suggested Keir might use his expertise to start the craft centre in Penbridge.'

There was a silence as Erica put her hand on Keir's arm and said, 'Nina Ellison was my sister. We were very different people, but Hugh's project was dear to my heart and Keir and I hope to set up some sort of trust for young people, as part of the project.'

Sophie wanted to go to Keir and put her arms about him, knowing how difficult it must have been for him to have shared all this, but she realised that now was not the occasion.

# All in the Past

It was two weeks later. Erica had concluded her business and returned to Spain.

Sophie and Keir were sitting in the study at Rowanbank. It was a mild March day and the daffodils were already beginning to raise their golden heads.

Keir sighed with pleasure. 'I love this time of year. The promise of spring with new life about to burst forth. The craft centre is on schedule for the grand opening just after Easter. Do you think Rose could be persuaded to display her dolls' house furniture there?'

Sophie smiled. 'I think she might agree to that. She's feeling much happier about things now.'

Sophie leant against Keir's large, comforting frame. 'There is still one thing that puzzles me.'

'What's that, my love?'

'I suspect there was something a little deeper than the refurbishment of this house that caused the rift between Erica and Aunt Rose.'

Keir looked at her and smiled. 'Mmn — I know I'd never be able to keep any secrets from you, Sophie. You see Rose had always hoped Hugh would marry her one day.'

Sophie's head shot up. 'After Uncle Tom died, you mean?'

'Well, naturally, but you see, she'd always loved Hugh, but he chose Mary. Tom adored Rose and so, after Hugh and Mary were married, Tom proposed and I'm sure they had a happy life together. Much later, after their respective partners had died, Rose hoped Hugh might marry her, but he just didn't love her — not in that way.'

Sophie stared at Keir as his words sank in. 'And Erica knew this?'

Keir nodded. 'Hugh told her, probably unwisely. He'd had no idea Erica would behave in the way she did towards Rose and he confided in me. The problem was, I could see both sides. You must realise that Erica really did love Hugh and they were happy together.'

'Poor Aunt Rose! That's so sad!' Sophie said. 'I'd no idea.'

Keir stood up. 'Shall we go in the garden? It's going to be an absolute picture when the blossom comes out.'

He took Sophie's hands and pulled her up, entwining an arm about her waist. 'I love this garden!' Sophie enthused. 'Everything's golden at the moment — the forsythia, the mahonia, the daffodils.'

Keir drew her to him and gave her a long, lingering kiss.

'What did I tell you about the promise of spring?' he murmured against her hair. 'Sophie Burnett, I love you, my own golden girl. You've made me come alive again and I want you to live with me here in this beautiful house. So will you marry me?'

'Oh yes, Keir. Yes,' she whispered, her

eyes shining as she reached up and kissed him.

They stood locked in an embrace beneath the apple tree at the bottom of the garden, listening to a blackbird as it heralded spring.

## THE END